The Knights and The Table

by

Anthony Buckley

Best wishes

Anthony Buckley

Vicar,

St Michael at the
North Gate
Oxford

New Generation Publishing

Chapter 1: The Queen and the Knight 1

Chapter 2: The Quest is Renewed 8

Chapter 3: The King Returns 16

Chapter 4: A Story Begins to be Retold 25

Chapter 5: Coming Home? 34

Chapter 6: Finding the Right Song 39

Chapter 7: An Archery Contest 49

Chapter 8: The Courage of Annabel 56

Chapter 9: Staying Patient, Staying Thankful 63

Chapter 10: Glastonbury 71

Chapter 11: The Wolves Are Coming Near 80

Chapter 12: Taking a Seat at the Table 88

Chapter 13: Letting Excalibur Go 95

Chapter 14: History Need Not Repeat Itself 101

Chapter 1

The Queen and the Knight

The meeting was going rather well; he had been able to dispose of the question without it being answered. When the break for lunch arrived, the Headmaster slipped outside. It was a fine summer morning. He paused for a moment in the fresh air, listening to the birds singing.

He was satisfied with the progress so far, and allowed himself a small, private smile. He looked at his watch. A couple more items on the agenda and then the rest of the afternoon was free.

If he had known what two people inside the room were saying he would not have allowed himself the smile.

"I have enjoyed the meeting so far," the new Governor, Mr Vincent, was saying. "There are many interesting things I need to think about. Thank you for the way you are leading us through."

The Chairman nodded modestly, wrestled his attention from the question of which sandwich to choose next, and replied: "It is good to have you here; we always like to have a new member on the Board here at St. George's. Do always ask if there is anything we can make more clear. Please do, always, please do." He turned back to the food trays.

"That is very kind," said Mr Vincent. "Thank you so much. There is one thing I would like to revisit after lunch if we may. It is about the proposal in the last item and the Headmaster's response."

The Chairman was slightly surprised at the assertiveness in Mr Vincent's voice; after all, this was only his first meeting. However, to alienate a new Governor might end up being unhelpful. He agreed to return to the item, but gently made clear that only a couple of minutes could be spent going over old ground. Mr Vincent was suitably appreciative and was effusive in his thanks.

Lunch was finished. The Governors and Headmaster returned to the table. The Chairman began: "Mr Moore, I am sorry to bring us back to a previous discussion but before we move to the next item on the agenda, I wondered if you could kindly very briefly explain again your thinking about the possible post for Mr Ladd?"

The Headmaster looked across at him.

I do not understand why you are doing this, he wanted to say, coldly and ruthlessly, but he knew he could not. He sensed that a breeze was unexpectedly, momentarily, blowing from a different direction. He was not quite sure where it had come from but his mind was as sharp as ever. He would adjust his sails because he knew one day he would be running with a stronger wind. He could live with this interruption.

He spoke carefully: "I will of course be happy to re-open the discussion, if my idea of referring it to a committee does not meet with everyone's approval?" And he looked slowly and steadily at each face around the table.

Through various smiles and shaking of heads those present made it clear that they had no desire to put the Headmaster to any trouble. Except one. The new Governor met his gaze and spoke: "I understand that your hesitation was financial, Mr Moore. You said that you had nothing personally against this person joining the staff but you needed to consider the costings. Whatever the costs are, I have decided that I will cover them and I propose to the Chairman and to the Board that we accept this offer from one of our foremost music journalists, Gary Ladd, former pupil at this school, to join our staff as a scholar in residence for one term."

Ed Moore sensed he was in danger of being out-manoeuvred. In the earlier discussion he had set aside other possible arguments and had focused on the cost issue, thinking that this would sway the decision and enable him to leave this question untouched and postponed. He looked at Mr Vincent and sensed that this new governor could be a powerful player. Best to go with the breeze, sidestep the fight and appear to win. Achieve the draw so as not to be later checkmated.

"I am so, so, grateful and relieved," he said. "Mr Ladd would indeed be such a good addition to the team. And I am extremely thankful to Mr Vincent for his generous offer. Thank you very much indeed. Excellent. Are we agreed?"

The Chairman, somewhat confused by the change of tone, accepted the proposal. It was passed without dissent. The Headmaster smiled broadly and stayed robustly cheerful through the rest of the meeting.

***

Three days later he was looking at a message delivered by hand to his study.

"You will explain to me how you allowed this to happen. He is coming. We do not know why. But – I cannot make this plainer – he will need to be destroyed."

Ed Moore read it again. No names. No courtesy. So much taken for granted. The usual mix of threat, anger and command. He leant back in his chair, gazed at the narrow rectangular table that stretched in front of him to the door, and closed his eyes.

There were moments when it all seemed so tedious and unimportant. He had not been in control of the decision at the meeting as he would have wished; he was now having to look at notes with instructions which carried no explanation. He allowed the reverie to continue for a few moments more. Was his heart going out of the fight? Why must Gary Ladd be destroyed? It all felt like a game, and he was beginning to wonder whether he was being treated as a piece on the board rather than a player. And that he had little idea who was really setting the rules.

He screwed up the paper that carried the message, and let it fall to the floor.

Two minutes later he bent over and picked it up and put it safely in a pocket.

One can't be too careful.

***

As a new Governor, Mr Vincent was expected to visit the school and he arrived for his tour later that month. Two pupils were assigned to show him around. He was courteous, interested, purposeful and friendly. He asked appropriate questions and was appreciative of all he saw.

As they were returning to the front entrance at the end of the tour he said quickly and firmly, "Thank you so much. I am just going upstairs to see one of the classrooms again. You can go to your lessons. Thank you."

The pupils looked at each other. They had expected to walk their visitor back to the school entrance, but they understood that a Governor had some sort of status and authority, although they were not sure what. Could he simply go and wander somewhere else? They surely were not meant to contradict him? In their moment of hesitation, Mr Vincent had left them behind.

Mr Moore came around the corner. He looked at the pupils. His eyes flashed.

"Where did he go?" The pupils froze and floundered for words. He did not wait for an answer.

"Did he go upstairs?"

The pupils nodded.

The Headmaster stepped forward, genuine anger in his eyes. And then he stopped. He turned around and quietly said, "You may go now." And so they went, wondering what all this was about and deciding that old Moore must be having a bad day. But Ed Moore stood still in the corridor, with a curious mix of fading anger and heavy-heartedness but also assurance, almost relief, that the battle was openly afoot.

On the top floor, at the end of the corridor, Mr Vincent paused in front of a classroom. He glanced again at the number above it and smiled: Room 868. He opened the door.

"You are welcome," said a voice.

"Thank you, and that still means more to me than I can express. I do not deserve the welcome." He stepped forward. And then paused and bowed slightly. "Guinevere, it is an honour to see you. I have never seen you in a school before. I think it suits you."

The classroom was empty except for Jenny Loss, a long-term teacher at St. George's. She was sitting towards the back. She smiled. "Welcome fair Lancelot. It has been a long time indeed. Are you ready for the quest?"

He moved closer and sat next to her. "May I ask what it is?"

"When we are asked if we are ready for a quest, it is usually more honourable to answer before knowing what the quest entails. You know that."

"That may usually be true, but it depends on who is doing the asking. But, dear Queen, as it is you, then I will say yes."

He looked at her and she caught a glimpse of the strength and vitality in his eyes that had once meant so much to her in so many different ways. She smiled. And she knew that he understood why she was smiling. So many mistakes, so many mistakes, but the restoration and the understanding had been deep and complete. That chapter was long gone and the new one had been very good. The past had not been repeated. And so she said simply: "Gary is coming back to the school this week, you played your part in achieving this and we thank you. We must try and protect him."

"His quest continues?"

"His quest continues."

"Protected from whom?"

"Protected from those who fear what he will do to people's minds. And they have designs on the Grail. They have no idea what it means, but they know it has a power outside their control, and so they want to destroy it."

"What can I do?"

"Be here as much as you can be, use your instincts. You know the values of our Order; you know them better than most.

"Oh, and Lancelot, when you said you do not deserve the welcome, you are right and you are wrong. You are right because no one *deserves* another's welcome; you are wrong if you think that friendship and forgiveness are conditional. We are welcome as we are, we are under grace. Don't try and sidestep the grace by feeling you need to earn the welcome." She sighed. "That has always been rather a failing."

Lancelot got up and bowed to his Queen. "I was right, being a teacher in a school does suit you." She stood up and laughed, and they embraced.

Chapter 2

The Quest is Renewed

A few days later Ed Moore was welcoming the new member of staff. He met him in the entrance hall and was careful of his words, conscious that others may be listening.

"Gary, Gary. How good to welcome you back. I was so pleased I could persuade the Governors to agree to your appointment. You will remember where the music department is, of course, from your days here as a pupil? But here is one of our brightest musicians, Annabel, to take you to your room and introduce you to your new colleagues on the way."

"What music do you like?" Gary asked Annabel, as they walked down the corridor.

"I like all kinds of music, as long as it has a strong tune."

"And what do you mean by a strong tune?"

She stopped, and looked rather startled.

"Don't worry," said Gary. "I am a journalist and old habits die hard. I like asking questions, and I like finding out about people. I am not testing you or trying to catch you out."

"I think I mean a tune that I cannot ignore, a tune that does something to how I feel," Annabel said, thoughtfully.

"And do you choose the music to reflect where you already are or do you choose music to take you to a different place?"

Again she looked slightly uncertain.

"My fault," said Gary. "Too many questions all at once. Let's keep walking."

"I don't mind the questions," said Annabel as they continued to walk. "I think I rather like them. It is just that I wasn't really expecting them."

She led the way to the music department and then said goodbye. Gary met the music teachers, familiarised himself again with the layout of the school and the newer buildings and was shown to an office which would be his temporary home. He realised that it was the same room where a teacher called Mark Lind had worked (albeit briefly) many years before.

He took a piece of paper from his pocket and unfolded it. He knew the words by heart but he enjoyed seeing them as well as remembering them. And this was the room, he guessed, where they had been written.

Did the hands that shape the cup know the meaning it would hold?
Or see the deepening stories that unendingly unfold?
The wine, the blood, the vision, the quest across the sea,
The strange and flowing riches that fashioned Glastonbury.

Did the hands that share the cup know the searching it would bring,
From knights and nameless pilgrims who wished to serve their king?
Did they sense the drawing power of all that lay within,
The fellowship, the sacrifice, of losing all to win?

He sensed that someone was near. Looking up, he saw the Headmaster standing in the doorway. Gary turned the paper over and laid it on the desk.

"Just called in to see if you are settling in," said Mr Moore. He looked around and said, rather coldly, "I did not know you were being given this room."

"I am settling in, thank you, everyone has been very kind," said Gary.

Ed Moore walked over, picked up the piece of paper and read it. He then turned as if to leave. Gary was surprised by the rudeness but was equally surprised that the Headmaster did not seem to mind how rude his action had appeared.

Mr Moore stopped at the door. Looking away from Gary, facing out of the room into the corridor, he asked: "Why do you want it so much?"

"Why do I want what so much?" asked Gary, calmly.

"This old relic, this cup, this Grail, whatever you want to call it."

"I do not know the complete answer to that. But I know that when searching for something good, a person tends to do good while searching. The Grail speaks of a great deal of goodness. The destination might shape the journey. My calling is to search for the Grail, and so I do."

"Stick to your job while you are here, which I imagine will not be very long. And I want no mention of this idiocy here. We are a modern school with no interest in being lost in fantasies."

"You may think I am lost in fantasies. What are you lost in, Mr Moore?"

The Headmaster turned back into the room. He took a pace forward and spoke fiercely: "You had your chance to join us when we offered you the deal last year. You turned us down. We do not forgive, that is not our style. I don't know what game you are playing that made you think you should be back here."

He took another step forward. "Don't push me. Remember where power lies."

Gary smiled. "I wonder if you know."

Ed Moore went to the desk, picked up the paper and tore it to pieces. He left the room.

***

Ed Moore guessed that the visit would not be long in coming. When, some days later, his secretary told him that Mr Le Fay had arrived, Ed immediately cancelled a meeting with some pupils and welcomed him to his study. Mr Le Fay was tall, unsmiling and immaculately dressed. He leant across the table and asked: "You got my note. You know how I feel. What went wrong?"

"The new Governor, Vincent, managed to persuade the Chairman to raise the issue again. He paid for the post. What else could I do?"

"I am not here to waste time guiding or advising you, I am here to tell you what the end result needs to be and I judge your effectiveness by your ability to obey successfully. *How* you obey is of no interest to me. I told you that we did want him here. His reasons for pulling out of the arrangement last year are still unclear to us, he could have made a lot of money out of helping us. He has chosen not to help us, and we must find different ways of increasing our influence in this country. We want power, Mr Moore. We are needed to bring order and wealth and control. The media world, the political world, are ours for the taking if we can influence enough people. Gary Ladd is not on our side, he might be dangerous."

Ed shrugged. "I can't see what harm he can do. He is only one, I can make him look inadequate. I can neutralise him. He won't be here for long."

"Don't underestimate him. Why has he wanted to come back? Who is he going to influence? We do not know his plans."

"He has got nothing."

"It is not what he *has*, it is what he *is*, and what drives him, that may be the problem. And what he might be part of."

Le Fay looked down and traced his hands across the table. "The table in this room was not always this shape. Remember that. Don't take anything for granted."

"Arthur is long gone," said Ed.

Le Fay looked up, and said coldly: "Is he?"

***

In morning assembly, the next day, Mr Moore said to the school, "You may not know that when Mr Ladd, our new, temporary, esteemed music assistant in residence, was here as a pupil the school had an unusual and strange post called Storyteller and Poet. The teacher who occupied that post was someone called Mr Lind. Not a great success, I am sorry to say, and he had to leave within a term. As Mr Ladd is with us in assembly today I am going to ask him to give us a poem. Just like Mr Lind would have done (although hopefully a little better). Mr Ladd, the floor is yours."

Gary gazed calmly from his seat near the back. He did not write poems. The Headmaster knew he did not. He had not been given any warning and was being set up to fail. The pupils waited expectantly; Gary got up and walked towards the raised stage. He stood in front of it, the Headmaster sat above and behind him on the stage itself.

He looked around to face the pupils and said, "Thank you, Headmaster, for your welcome this morning. I indeed was a pupil when Mr Lind taught here. The Headmaster in those days was someone called Mr English. Things were indeed a little unusual. But here we are in the present and it is a pleasure to be back. Thank you for your welcome. I am a music journalist and so know a little more about music than I do about poetry.

"But we can say that all poetry is music. All poems have a rhythm or tune, and perhaps what the poet is doing is allowing the reader to share in the task of putting the words to music. And we all choose our own music. Each one of you will read a poem in a different way to me.

"I do not usually write poems, but sometimes I catch myself wondering why some places or situations affect me more deeply than I expect. As the Headmaster has asked me to give a poem, here is an attempt to express this feeling. It is my offering to you this morning. When you are next in a place that speaks deeply, you may remember it, or the feelings behind it. Here it is, a poem for special moments:

What is it here that opens doors
And glimpses further lands
That speaks of other, distant, shores
And journeys not yet made?

What is it here that draws me in
And calls my searching heart
That lifts my eyes from narrow roads
To wider, gentler, paths?

What is it here that catches me
With beauty beyond words
That speaks of life, unshackled, free
Where dreams are rich, and heard?

He stopped, bowed slightly to the pupils, and walked back to his seat.

Ed Moore watched him: *he is not afraid, this is why he is dangerous, he is not scared. When Lind was here, he was afraid. We marginalised him quite easily; we don't know what effect his feeble poems and stories may have had, but probably very little or none. But Gary Ladd, even after what he did, or nearly did, last year, is not afraid. Still, his attempt at a poem will not have caused any damage. Not easy to grasp what he was trying to say. But I should not have risked asking him; that was a mistake.*

He finished the assembly with some notices and dismissed the school to their lessons.

He watched Gary leave the hall and then followed him to his room.

"Mr Ladd," he said abruptly. "You need to be more scared of me. You know that I know all about last year, your nasty little plan to blackmail a former friend and to join with us. Even though you pulled back from that, you behaved very badly. I hold that knowledge over you, and you should be afraid. I might begin to drip some rumours here and there."

"That season when I behaved so badly no longer has power over me," said Gary. "My friend has forgiven me. I am free from the fear as I am free from the guilt. You cannot touch me."

"The one who is supposed to be able to find this nonexistent Grail is meant to be perfect. You are rather a long way from that."

"We have different definitions of perfection."

"You are a failed journalist who struggles to find a job and ends up giving a few hours a week to a third-rate school."

"We have different definitions of failure."

"If someone like you can find the so-called Grail, anyone can."

"Yes, that's rather exciting, isn't it?"

Ed Moore turned and left the room. Le Fay was right. He had to get rid of Ladd. He was beginning to be rather annoying.

Chapter 3

The King Returns

Mark Lind had indeed briefly worked at the school ten years before. A year ago there had been a reunion for some of the pupils and teachers involved in that term's events. Through this reunion Mark had renewed contact with Emma Armstrong and they were now chatting at a café near the school. Their table was near the door, near the coats and the coming and going of customers, but it was not too noisy and Emma was quietly reading aloud from a notebook.

They say, they say, that I have failed.
That I'm not good enough.
Ceaselessly the voices cry
Constantly they cry

And still they cry and cry and cry
That I'm not good enough.

And who are you
to say they're wrong?
Who are you
to think I'm strong?

She looked up.

"That's how it is, that is it. That is my attempt at a poem for today," she said. "I do not fully understand, and no one fully understands, why I feel the way I do. We guess the causes as much as we want, but our guesses will never be completely right. I do not know why those voices, that say I am no good, are so strong."

"Whose are the voices?" said Mark.

"No one in particular, too many to mention, just life," said Emma. She shrugged. "Do you think I'll ever be a poet?"

"I think we are all poets, no one thinks or speaks purely in prose. Whether we write poems is a different question. As you will remember, I am not good at writing them, but it seems that there was a time when I was called to do so, whatever the quality. I think that you might well be called to do so, too. I like this one, although the rhyme in the last part was almost too powerful, as if the directness of the wrong/strong distracted from the meaning itself?"

"Then why did you like it?"

"Because you were able to communicate something that you felt, something that you wanted to say. I think that art is all about communication. And therefore your poem worked."

"You seem much more confident about all this than you used to be," said Emma. "It seems as if you are really are growing to become more like Merlin. Perhaps that is how it works: we are given the cloak, and then grow into it."

"I don't feel very Merlin-ish today." Mark smiled. "In fact I seldom do."

"I suspect Arthur would say that this is why you are good at it. It's about what you are, not what you feel." She paused. "What are you thinking?"

Mark said, "I am thinking about your voices, and that has started me thinking about the voices that trouble me. I look back and remember the moments that nobody else would realise were significant to me, but these are the ones that are etched in my mind. These moments all contained something about friendship and hope and the feeling that that one day all would be well. So much of the rest of my life has been unconsciously or consciously committed to repeating those moments. And that was a mistake. Because appreciation, not repetition, is the right desire. It is not the moments themselves that matter, it is what they point towards."

"Where do the voices come in?"

"Sometimes the voices say I am foolish to value the moments at all, that I should forget the longings they touched. And that call to forget, even to despise, those memories and those longings, come from voices that I don't think are on my side."

"Perhaps we both need to listen to better voices," said Emma.

Mark nodded, and then asked: "Are you still in touch with any of the others?"

"Not really. I know that Gary is back at St. George's. Some temporary role helping in the music department."

"Is that wise?"

Emma was about to answer when her eye was caught by someone who had come through the door. He was carefully taking off his scarf and putting it on a peg. While still looking at the coat hooks, he spoke. He did not speak loudly, but his voice carried through the clatter of customers and crockery.

"It is wise because he obeyed the call to do it. Whether it is sensible or safe in the world's eyes is another matter and rather less important." He turned and faced the table, still holding a coat. "Good morning, dear Emma and dear

Mark, may I join you?"

The former Headmaster of their school pulled up a chair and sat beside his old colleague and pupil. Emma looked at him and her face was shining.

"Mr English, you're back?" she asked.

"I am back," Rex English replied. "I am never very far away, you know. And it is a pleasure to see you both again."

"Does the fact that you are back mean that something is happening?" Emma continued.

"Something is always happening." He smiled. "But you are right, there is a particular task that I may be of some help with, by being, shall we say, a little more obviously present than I usually am."

He continued: "Gary is indeed back at St. George's. The ripples of his being there may yet affect some individuals quite strongly. And so our enemies do not want him there."

"Is that because he is planning to do something or because they always see him, and I suppose us, as a problem. Why do we matter to them?" asked Emma.

"There is nothing that Gary does that would truly hurt them, quite the opposite. They do not understand that. But they rightly sense that his presence challenges them. First, they and we cannot both be right in how the world is seen and nobody likes to be called wrong; if we are right it will mean they have to reconsider their priorities, their values and ambitions, and it is always more comfortable to stay with the familiar. Second, their financial interests might be damaged if they lose people to our side; remember, they were not pleased when Gary pulled out of their scheme last year. Third, they have grown accustomed to being the centre of influence, that is where their sense of self-worth comes from. To learn that the world does not revolve around them and their views may be difficult for them to handle."

"Can't they just leave us in peace?" asked Emma. "Why the need to keep fighting?"

"They do not have the contentment to allow others to be content. And they like their influence over people; never forget, dear Emma, that power can become addictive. They enjoy being in control and have difficulty giving that up. To be fair, we do not want to leave them entirely in peace either; they may wish to crush us, but we want to challenge and change them."

Mr English paused. "Have you heard of the phrase 'to be scared out of your wits'?"

"Yes, but not often, it feels a bit old-fashioned."

"Do you know what it means?"

"I've never really thought about it. Something about forgetting your understanding?"

"You are on the right track but it is more complex. Centuries ago, the word 'wits' carried specific meanings. There were five inward wits to match the five outward 'senses', the ones which we can easily name – hearing, smell, touch, taste and sight. The five inward wits were sometimes described as *Common sense, Imagination, Fantasy, Estimation* and *Memory. Common sense* was similar in meaning to our modern use, but included especially the ability to behave sensibly when with others, acting sensibly to build up the community: community sense, common sense. *Imagination* was the ability to imagine what is named, so if someone says 'four-legged table' you are able to picture a 'four-legged table' in your mind. *Fantasy* was the ability to imagine an object that you may not have seen, for example, a seven-legged table. *Estimation* was about being able to react instinctively in a wise, not destructive, way, the capacity to react well even if you do not really have time to think. *Memory* was the vital ability to remember clearly what has truly helped and what has truly hindered; people forget the past surprisingly often.

"There are people, and the Le Fay family is a good example, who want people to forget their wits, to be witless, dim-witted, to be a nothing-wit, a nit-wit; this is now used as a childish insult but the underlying meaning is quite strong. They do not want people to think and remember clearly. They want them to lose their ability to react appropriately. They do not want them to be accurate in their understanding or in their imaginings. They want people not to know or care how to behave with common sense, with sense in community, because good communities would threaten their divisive rule. The Le Fays want robots who will only think as they are told to think. Dictators always want their people to be witless.

"They want to be the only ones whose views matter. And this has consumed them so much that they now want everyone to sing their song, even though the song is a dreary one. They want people to think the way they do and are frustrated if they do not. They are like children who want to control their circle of friends, they cannot bear the idea of people thinking independently, of being free, of making their own choices.

"And they want the Grail."

"Why?" asked Mark.

"Because they think that if they can destroy it then they will have destroyed the stories around it, and the attraction these stories have for people. And they think, rather childishly, that in destroying it they will upset Gary (and others) and this in itself will satisfy some of their spite."

There was quiet for a few moments, and Mark asked: "What do you want us to do?"

"As always with our enemies, we hope to win them, to soften their attitudes, to widen their vision, to allow them the freedom not always to control others. We want them to become friends. But we must face the fact that we may not win them, so instead we must prepare to reduce their influence by protecting people from their voices. We must keep telling the right stories, speaking the right poetry, singing the right songs."

"I am happy to play my part again," said Mark.

"I know that you are, and I thank you, but you would not be welcome back at St. George's. Ed Moore was able to get rid of you when he got rid of me all those years ago and he will keep the door shut. This is not your time. But Emma is a different person, and she has already shown that something of Merlin rests in her. Emma could go to St. George's."

"Mr English, Arthur," said Emma, slowly. "I am not in a good place at the moment. As Mark knows, I'm finding things tough. The reunion last year helped, but I am not there yet. Others will help you better."

"Emma," said Mr English. "If, through the centuries, I had waited for people always 'to be in a good place' before they took on a quest, nothing would ever have got done. Dragons would not have been slain, the needy would not have been helped, the vulnerable would not have been rescued. I am sad for you that you are feeling sad, but I have faith in what you can do, however you are feeling. I trust you, and I trust what you bring to the task. I am asking you to trust yourself, too."

"Will I have any help?" said Emma, rather shortly. "It would be nice if I did. I feel I've fought enough battles on my own."

"Not only nice, but essential," answered Mr English. "I do not choose people who will not ask for help. Yes, you will find friends there. Jenny Loss is still on the staff, Room 868 is still a meeting place for those of the Table. There is a new Governor, Mr Vincent, who is one of us. Unexpected allies may yet arise to help. Emma, you can be invited in as an former pupil. You are thinking of becoming a teacher and a request to observe lessons in the English department would not be out of place. And there you will help us."

"How?"

"By telling stories and poems as Mark did when he was there. And perhaps distracting attention away from Gary."

"And me?" asked Mark. "What do I do while this is happening?"

"Your task is to wait while the story unfolds. Mark, it is not easy to wait well. It is not easy to sit and watch when you have gifts you want to use. Your growth in patience is a quest in itself."

"Mr English," said Emma. "Before you came in I was telling Mark I thought he was becoming more like Merlin. Listening to you, I feel you are becoming more like Arthur."

Rex English smiled. "I am Arthur and I have always been so. But how much Arthur appears to people depends to some extent on how much that person is ready to see."

"To *some* extent?" said Emma.

"To some extent," said Mr English. "Only to some extent." He paused. "And that, Emma, was a very perceptive question, you have always been good at those. Now, are you willing to accept this calling?"

"Is this a calling?"

"It is."

"I accept, and…" She smiled at Mr English, "…and thank you."

Chapter 4

A Story Begins to be Retold

Ed Moore had not remembered that Emma Armstrong had known Gary Ladd at school. Their only link had been through Mark Lind when he had taught there, and Ed had not been aware of that connection. He likewise did not know about the later reunion. He thus thought very little about her request to come and observe for a month in the English department and agreed quickly. She began the next week.

After an introductory conversation with the Head of English she was ushered into a class halfway through a lesson.

"Have you any particular interest, Miss Armstrong?" asked Mr Aldwyn, the teacher.

Emma looked nervously round the faces. "Thank you. Good morning, everyone. I am interested in how particular stories seem to keep on being retold. Whether in books, poems, films, television series, plays and pantomimes – the same stories keep coming back."

"Have you any favourites?" asked Mr Aldwyn.

"I have always liked Robin Hood."

Mr Aldwyn was a friendly and popular teacher, but he was a little forgetful and his planning was not always the best. He had not remembered that Emma was due in to his lesson. He had fifteen minutes left and did not quite know what to do. He had been on the point of asking for some silent reading to fill the time, but he knew that would now not quite work. He seized the opportunity.

"Excellent, excellent. Why don't you give us all a taste of how you would tell something from the Robin Hood stories? My plans for the rest of the lesson can wait." He smiled benevolently at the pupils and then at Emma.

Emma looked at him blankly and was momentarily terrified. But she remembered Rex English's words in the café: this was what she was called to do, however she felt about it. There was an empty desk at the front of the classroom. She sat on it, smiled at the pupils around the room, and began:

Coming back, coming back.

Robin Locksley looked across the valley. He was coming back, and he was not sure what he would find.

He had been away for five years. He had seen great courage and profound sacrifice. He had seen strong leadership which had been deeply flawed. He had been inspired and disappointed, victorious and defeated. He had made some rich friendships. He looked behind him.

"Tuck?"

Friar Tuck rode up beside him. He wore a long dark cloak; if he were carrying a sword, it was hidden. A third rider joined them.

"We have looked over many valleys," said Tuck simply. "This is another one. We will go down and then we will go up."

The third rider laughed: "Is that the sort of profound, inspired and thoughtful wisdom we bring a Friar along to give? I am glad all that monastery training was so useful."

Robin smiled. "Yes, it is. And yes, it was. Come on, Will, come on all of us. Down into the valley."

There were three of them in the group: Robin Locksley, Friar Tuck and Will Scathlock. They guided their horses forward; the walk became a trot and then a canter, almost a gallop, as if the journey had taken on a new joy, a new importance and vitality. A mile across the valley stood a small hill and on the top was a castle. The riders were halfway along the track towards the hill when three figures stepped out fifty yards in front of them. Robin raised his hand and his companions slowed and stopped. He looked at the foremost figure, smiled, and dismounted.

"Marian," he said, and bowed slightly. "It has been a long time. Who are your friends?"

"These are Alan Dale and John Forrest," the lady replied. "Greetings, Robin. We heard you were coming back, and we guessed that you would be reaching the valley this morning. Let me speak plainly: you are thinking of going back to your castle; it is no longer yours. Gisborne has taken it. And he has imposed new laws. I can't think how many you have broken already this morning by arriving on horseback, wearing swords, and no doubt thinking all the wrong things. Speaking of which, that one looks like some sort of Friar (here Tuck bowed with a smile); well, he won't do at all. Gisborne doesn't do that sort of thing." She smiled. "It is good to see you all. Robin Locksley, welcome home. It is a shame it is no longer your home."

"I'm coming back," said Robin. "And it will be my home again. I may need your help."

"Robin Locksley, asking for help? Things have changed."

"I have learned much in my time away. Now tell me, Marian, what help could you give, if you were so minded."

"John here is strong, very strong, he has the strength of five men when he is roused. Alan sings songs, can warm hearts and bring comfort. And as for me, I want revenge, do not ask me why. And I will get it. As to your two, I am not sure what help a Friar could be, but the fact that Gisborne won't like him is good enough for me. Who is the other one?"

"This is Will Scathlock. He can send arrows wherever they need to go and is a fine swordsman. We are six, shall we go forward?"

"We are enough, and this further help I will give: I will guide you as to what we should do. I was always a better thinker than you were, Robin, or has the impulsive young man grown up in his time away?"

Tuck laughed. "It is always a risk returning home, Robin, people know you too well." He swung down from his horse. "Maiden Marian, Robin of Locksley has seen Jerusalem, he has acted with courage and honour to friend and foe. He is coming back and Gisborne should tremble. Yes, you are right, he is as impulsive as ever. But now it is deepened and enriched with strength and wisdom. His wits grow stronger. Lead us, maiden, let us go forward."

Emma paused. She did not know if the pupils were enjoying the story. She felt increasingly anxious. She glanced behind her, Mr Aldwyn looked at his watch.

"Please continue, Miss Armstrong. We only have a few minutes left, anyway."

Emma took a deep breath and began again, trying to focus on the faces of those who looked as if they were listening.

Guy of Gisborne sat in the great hall of the castle. One day he would knock it down and start again, but at the moment

28

it amused him to be sitting where the Locksley family had once sat. He was a strong and handsome man. He liked, literally and metaphorically, to dress up in Locksley robes and to despise them at the same time. It was his weekly meeting, in front of him were representatives of the village. He smiled at Marian. She did not smile back. Behind her stood five men. Two, John Forrest and Alan Dale, he knew. The other three he did not; one looked normal enough and one had a hood pulled down so his face could hardly be seen. He must have some skin disease, thought Guy, who could not imagine being seen in public with his face looking less than perfect. The last wore a monk's habit. Guy grimaced. One day, all that will go, he promised himself.

"I wish to bring some order to this rather chaotic and slovenly village," he said in his most languid voice, and looked behind him for nods from his guards. He turned forward again but there were no answering smiles among the villagers. He noticed this, but was not concerned. "I want everyone to report to me at this time every week to tell me how their craft, trade or farming is going. We will discuss targets for the week ahead. Those who meet their targets will have nothing to fear; indeed, I will be pleasant to them."

"Will this new system make us happy?" a voice rang out.

Silence filled the hall. Gisborne paused and he looked more thoughtful. His gaze slowly swept across the faces, gauging reactions, checking for signs. The eyes behind the hood met his but were expressionless. Gisborne pondered. There was something here he did not quite understand. He simply said: "The maid Marian and I will talk for a moment, the rest of you stay here." He gestured to his guards, who stood more alert and gazed watchfully at the villagers.

He ushered Marian out of the hall into a corridor and roughly pushed the door behind them. She turned and faced him. He spoke roughly: "It is people like you that remind me why I need to do what I need to do. I know what the sheriff wants. I know the control the prince wants. People like you get in the way. Your rudeness just now will not be forgotten."

"But you can't get rid of me easily, can you," answered Marian. "Remember, the true king will return. And my question was the right one: will your changes make people happier? Not, Guy, will it make you feel more important. Will it make them happier?"

"You ask the wrong questions and you do not see things as they are. The king will not come back. And you will learn to be scared. That's your problem at the moment, you don't know when you should be afraid."

She smiled. "So we know where we are. How different things might have been if you had been equally honest two years ago. But you are wrong, Guy, you are not going to win. You think you will, you may even think you do, but you will not win. There is nothing now that you can do that scares me. You have done your worst. And I am still standing. You are the one who has lost."

"We will see," he said, but there was little power in the words.

He turned back towards the hall and it was then that they both noticed that the door was ajar. His earlier slamming must have been too hard and it had bounced back open. They looked at each other with a moment of understanding that they might have been heard and that might yet matter.

"It is too late for secrets, Guy, anyway," said Marian. "Everything becomes known in the end." She stood back

so that he could enter the hall first. The sight that met them caused Gisborne to stop sharply.

His guards were facing the wall, their faces so close that their noses were almost touching the stones. They were being watched by Will Scathlock, bow in one hand, arrow in the other, and John Forrest, who was leaning against his heavy wooden staff. The other man, now with his hood pulled back, walked towards Gisborne.

"Well, Guy," he said. "I have come back."

The bell rang.

"Oh, I'm terribly sorry, Mr Aldwyn," said Emma. "I have used up all your time."

Mr Aldwyn replied warmly, and then tried to look slightly regretful: "That is no problem at all, no problem at all. I am sure I can catch up another time and sadly, class, there is no time to set homework, you must go now."

The pupils set off in a rush.

"Thank you so much, Emma," said Mr Aldwyn. "You must come again in the next lesson. I am sure the pupils enjoyed your story, and of course it is so useful for them to hear about our literary roots."

Later that morning Mr Moore bumped into Mr Aldwyn in the corridor. "Is Emma Armstrong settling in? It would be good for our reputation if former pupils felt comfortable coming back."

"She seems to be settling in. She came in and told a story about Robin Hood. The children seemed to enjoy listening to her."

"I have to keep telling you. They are not children, they are pupils. Anyway, what part of the story?"

"The beginning, about Robin Locksley coming back. Reasserting authority."

The Headmaster went back to his office, thought for a moment, and asked his secretary to bring in some files from the archives. He placed them on his desk and flicked through them. *So, Miss Armstrong,* he said to himself, *you were here with Gary Ladd, and both when Mark Lind was here. And you are telling stories, as Lind used to do. I may have had the wrong instinct about you, you are perhaps not as unimportant as I had thought. And the Robin Hood story has a power of its own, whoever is doing the telling.* Ed Moore looked up and said aloud to the empty room: "Arthur, is this you? What are you planning?"

And at that moment he felt a tang of loneliness. These were his enemies and he knew he despised them and wanted to crush them. But suddenly it struck him that his own circle was not very attractive, that it was characterised by fear and control. He realised he did not like his master. The Arthur circle he was facing seemed to have a sense of belonging and affection. It seemed also to be quite mixed and fluid, unexpected people were part of it and they each came to it as they were. Arthur's kingship seemed to liberate, not enslave. His mind continued to roam. Jenny Loss, he had always wondered if she were part of it. And presumably Mr Vincent, it was he who had got Gary Ladd installed. *How many of them are there?*

And then the moment passed. His mind was brought back to its normal channels. He was in control. Who needed a messy, disorganised group when you could have a tight and secure ring, led strongly, if ruthlessly, by a man like Le Fay? And he had got where he wanted. He had his own friends, whatever friendship means. Emma Armstrong was only here for a month. She could not do much harm in that time.

Chapter 5

Coming Home?

The pupils were rather bemused when Mr Aldwyn explained during the next lesson that Miss Armstrong was very keen to carry on telling her story, and that as she was only here for a few weeks it was courteous to give her time, but they were as happy listening to her stories as anything else, perhaps more so. Towards the end of the lesson Emma sat on her usual desk and continued:

Gisborne took in the sight that met his eyes. He reached for his sword but then heard Marian's voice behind him.

"Now, Guy, my knife is an inch from your back. Why do you think I let you go through the door first? Move your hand from your sword and proclaim, loudly, that you are leaving this house right now. And when you get out of knife-range from me, remember that one of my men is watching you from one of the shadows. His arrow is resting on the string. When you go, take your guards with you."

Guy of Gisborne shrugged his shoulders. His hand moved away from his sword. Still facing forward he quietly spoke, his voice was cruel and cold. "I will not forget this day and we will meet again. And remember, Marian, only cowards hold knives to people's backs."

Marian's face turned pale, but not with fear. She leaned forward, her knife pressing through his outer clothes and whispered fiercely: "One day you will know what the word coward means. One day, when you are a real man, you will understand what a coward you were. Now go."

Gisborne took a step forward, looked at the watching crowd in the hall, and announced he was leaving.

Emma glanced behind. Mr Aldwyn was sitting in his chair at his desk. At first she thought he was concentrating hard, she then wondered if he were dozing. She looked again at the class. One of the pupils smiled and mimed putting her cheek against her hands as though asleep and then mouthed, "Carry on with the story."

And so she did.

Gisborne strode out, John Forrest and Will Scathlock stood aside and the guards followed him.

Robin Locksley looked around at his beloved hall once again. He had waited long for this moment. He was home. The villagers stayed standing in the hall, respectfully waiting for words from their returned master.

"I am home, and I thank you," said Robin. "And you are always welcome here. This is my home, but it is also the home of the village." He looked across to the side of the hall and nodded.

Alan Dale stepped into the light from the shadows, bow still in hand, and began to sing, his clear voice filling the hall.

This place of dreams and memories
This place of hope and peace
of welcome love
that's shared with all
as happened long ago.

This place of warmth, of tears, of joy
Where we are held as one
Where we can rest
and sing and dance
As happened long ago.

This place for you, for me, for us
Where doors are opened wide
Can we rebuild
Can we restore
as happened long ago?

The bell rang. Mr Aldwyn looked puzzled for a moment, jumped to his feet, and then said: "Most interesting, most interesting, Miss Armstrong. See how the tale unfolds, class, see how it unfolds. Lots to think about, I'm sure. Very helpful to all our English studies." He gazed slightly anxiously at the pupils, but was reassured by their polite nods.

Emma smiled at the class and they smiled back.

Mr Aldwyn remained in the room when Emma and the pupils had left, and began tidying his desk. Somewhere, he was sure, was his mark book and timetable. He often could not quite remember what or who his next lesson involved. He was searching through the drawers and sensed someone in the doorway.

"I was just passing," came a voice.

He looked up, the Headmaster was standing there.

"How was your lesson?" Mr Moore asked.

"Ah, well, yes. I think it went well."

"I hope you are remembering my clear instructions for

how every lesson in this school should run."

"Of course, Headmaster."

"Because I heard the end of the story Miss Armstrong was telling the children and she even seemed to be singing some sort of song. We don't want too many stories and songs, do we?"

He stepped back from the doorway and went up the corridor.

"Why not?" said Mr Aldwyn, but only to himself. He rather liked stories and songs. He did not usually like to make a fuss but Mr Moore had irritated him. When the next class arrived (the mark book was still unfound, but that no longer mattered) they were surprised when his first question, even before they sat down, was "Do you like stories and songs? I do! Why are they important? Why do they matter?" The discussion lasted most of the lesson; later, at lunchtime, he went to the staff room, and there he talked to some of his colleagues.

Mr Moore had gone back to his study. There, to his astonishment, sitting in a chair by a window, was his predecessor, Rex English.

"It wasn't always like this, Ed," said Mr English, before Mr Moore had a chance to say anything. "Sit down for a moment."

Ed Moore sat in a chair by the window, not in his usual place behind the desk.

"I have no idea what is going on. You can't turn up like this. This is my room. You left years ago. This is totally out of order. You have no right to be here. What are you doing here?"

"Two points to begin with: when you say 'out of order', what 'order', whose 'order', do you mean? And no one has a 'right' to be anywhere, not me, not you. None of us owns anything at all. Sometimes we are invited to visit for a while, but if we accept, we hold in our hands an invitation, not a legal claim. That, Ed, is rather liberating, but we can leave those questions for another time. Forgive me for being pedantic.

"What am I doing here? I am here to unsettle you by reminding you of something that is now not far from the surface. The something is this: there was once a child who enjoyed stories, who used his imagination and loved the open world beyond the simply tangible. Stars and space, dreams and tales, songs and adventures, he loved them all. And then he changed, he felt that the only way to happiness was through money and control, status and success, influence over others, whether that influence was for good or ill. And that the only thing that was real was what could be touched or seen or counted. And so he stopped listening to stories, and he felt threatened if others were listening to stories, because those stories opened up part of him that he wanted to forget. And he entrusted himself instead to the Le Fay family. He thought he was part of them, not realising he was merely serving them. They do not include, they only enslave.

"Ed, you are invited back to the Round Table. It is a better shape than this one. Why am I here? I am here to welcome you home."

Ed Moore looked at Rex English, shook his head, stood up, and walked out of the room.

Chapter 6

Finding the Right Song

"Do you compose music as well as write about it?" Annabel asked.

She was standing in Gary's room, having been asked to deliver some music manuscript paper to him.

"I try to," answered Gary. "I would find it difficult to comment about other people's music if I did not have some understanding of what they go through to write it. Similarly, I sometimes sing songs, so I can share a little in the world of singers. Composers and performers are at the heart of music; those of us who write about them need some humility, to try a little at least to walk a mile in their shoes. What they do is much more difficult than what we do."

"I like singing," she said simply, and sat down.

Gary looked at her thoughtfully: "I think you do, too. There is something about singing which is bigger than the song itself; it reminds us that the world is broader and wilder and I sense in you that wider awareness, that wider thoughtfulness.

"A piece of music is always part of a context, it never stands quite alone: listening to bird song on a fresh summer's morning is different from listening to a recording through headphones in a window-less prison cell. Both will remind us of bird-song, but our feelings will be different as we listen. Not better or worse, but different. It is always interesting to ask: 'Where am I when I sing this song?' or 'Where am I when I hear this music?' And perhaps above all, 'Do I realise that I never sing completely alone?'"

Annabel looked puzzled.

Gary continued: "There is something about music that always connects. It can connect us with the mood we are in, or how we feel the world is. It can connect us with our past, bringing back memories of people or places. No song stands on its own; it always comes from somewhere or is going somewhere. The ancients talked about the music of the spheres, unheard but faintly sensed by mortal hearts. When we sing well we are in some way joining in with that great song. There is always music in the air."

"So when people talk about being in harmony with the world, that might almost be meant literally?"

"Exactly."

She looked at the clock. "I must go now, I have English. I imagine Miss Armstrong will be telling us more about Robin Hood, that is all we seem to be doing this week."

"Do you mind?"

"No, I rather like it. What I can't decide is whether Mr Aldwyn is simply allowing it to happen or deliberately wants it to happen."

"Do you know much about Saxon names?" Gary asked.

"Nothing at all. I am not very good at history, I suppose Harold must have been a Saxon name, and Alfred."

"So was Aldwyn." Gary smiled. "You better go now, thank you for calling in. Keep singing."

Mr Aldwyn had indeed invited Emma to his next lesson but explained that it was going to be in a much bigger room. There had been discussions and the English Department had decided that all the pupils in the year group should listen to her. (He did not mention that it had equally been decided not to tell the Headmaster of this new arrangement.) Emma took a deep breath, explained where the story had reached so far, and continued:

John Forrest was talking with Robin Locksley.

"Are you pleased to be home?" John was asking.

"Yes, it is good to be back," said Robin. "But Gisborne will not leave us in peace. He has powerful friends and we are not many to resist him if he attacks."

But Gisborne did not come in force against the castle. He took his revenge by attacking the villagers. Night raids, stealing, burning down cottages and each time a notice pinned to a tree or post. "As long as Robin Locksley is in my castle, these punishments will continue against all who are traitorously allowing him to stay." After a time, some of the villagers came to the castle and asked Robin to leave.

He met with John Forrest, Marian, Alan Dale, Will Scathlock, and Tuck. "What do you think I should do?"

"The villagers will suffer if you stay and they will suffer if you go," said Marian. "You are vulnerable if you remain; there are only six of us, without the villagers' support you would be hard-pressed when Gisborne's attention turns here. Let us go the forest. It will be difficult for Gisborne to find us. And there we might be able to achieve more by subtler means."

"I don't like the idea of running," said Robin. "Even with

41

only six, with good bolts on the doors and archers on the battlements we could hold them for a time."

"Only for a time," Tuck repeated, "and then we would be finished. And this one would not be a holy sacrifice for the sake of others, this one would be self-indulgent heroics. No one else would benefit from your death. If you leave the village Gisborne may or may not treat the people better. But with you dead there will be no possibility of protecting them. You are still needed, even if you are in hiding. And the true king expects you to hold firm. There may come a time when your death is needed, it is not now."

"Some would say I will look like a coward," Robin said.

"Only to those who will refuse to understand," said Marian. "Are theirs the voices you most need to hear?"

"So I am on my travels again."

"We are always travelling," said Tuck. "The question is what do we do in the places where we are sent, and in what frame of mind we travel."

"Do we really have to turn everything into a sermon?" said Robin, roughly. There was an uncomfortable silence.

Will Scathlock shrugged his shoulders: "Let's accept it; it is time to travel again. But this time not far. Let's go to the woods. Gisborne will not find us there, we can do more harm to him from there than trapped in here."

And so the small band left the castle early next morning. One or two villagers were awake and came to greet them and thank them.

"We won't forget this. You are doing this for us. One day all will be well. You will be back. Thank you." Children

came running out of the cottages to wave. The six were a noble sight: gentle and strong, warriors of the king.

"We are not going far," Robin said. "To the woods, that will then be our home and yours."

The villagers cheered.

And so Robin's mood lifted. "Let us be singing the right song this morning. Master Dale: what do you have for us?"

Alan smiled, the group stopped, he turned to face the villagers.

> *I never thought of myself as a song-writer*
> *But the words wouldn't come any other way*
> *With our hearts full of hope, and the sun in the sky*
> *And the dawn breaking on a new day.*
>
> *I never thought of myself as a song-writer*
> *But the music grows brighter and clear*
> *And the universe sings, and the people are glad*
> *With the friendships held firm and held near.*
>
> *I never thought of myself as a song-writer*
> *And there's fear and despair close at hand*
> *So we sing the right song and we share in the hope*
> *And with courage and grace we will stand.*

Emma looked down, she had not planned or meant or wanted to sing another song. She did not think she had a good voice and now felt embarrassed, even ashamed, especially in front of this larger group. *What must they all think of me? How have I ended up looking so foolish? Where are these songs coming from?*

A voice broke in, calm and strong. "It is so, so, good of

Miss Armstrong to give us such an authentic flavour of these ancient stories by including the songs. We would be much the poorer without them." It was Mr Aldwyn, speaking with an unaccustomed note of authority. "Miss Armstrong, I salute you, and urge you to continue. We are very grateful."

Emma turned and slowly nodded her thanks. And then continued:

It was two months later, Robin Locksley and his small band were sitting in a clearing in the woods, near the bottom of a slope leading down to a valley. They had begun to fashion a settlement; shelters were built, paths in the immediate area were cleared. A large oak tree stood in the centre of the clearing and conversations often took place in its shade. The forest was dense and large, if Gisborne were minded to search for them they would be difficult to find. Occasionally villagers, driven to near despair by Gisborne's actions, would try and seek them out. Usually Robin's scouts would come across them and bring them to the settlement, where they would be rested and refreshed. They might choose to stay or return home as they wished. And so news from the village was brought to Robin.

"Gisborne is raging around his castle, kicking over things, hitting servants, shouting at the smallest imagined failing," Marian was saying. "He is an angry man."

"He has got so much of what he wants," said Robin. "I cannot see why he is so angry. I have seen so much anger in recent years. Tuck, what is this all about? Forgive my temper yesterday."

Tuck smiled. "There is little to forgive; I am sometimes annoying, that is part of my job. And you are right, there is indeed much anger in the world. There always has been, it is a lazy shortcut, remember that Cain decided to kill his brother rather than face his own issues.

"I wonder if anger is always an expression of another feeling, that in reality it is never the very first emotion we feel, even when it appears very quickly. There is always an initial instance of hurt, injustice, frustration, fear or sadness, and that then turns to anger. Or a small event can trigger a deep sadness or frustration or memory, known only by the person themselves, and then the explosion of anger can be a shock indeed to everyone else.

"There can be anger that is appropriate – responding to injustice, for example, but even then we have to make sure the anger is expressed in a helpful way. There can be anger that sadly comes from grief, when we don't know what to do with the sense of loss and so lash out instead. There is anger that comes from fear or guilt, where it is used as a defence to keep anyone else, or our own thoughts, at bay. Or it can be a way for the insecure to exercise power over others. If Gisborne is kicking chairs as well as people then it is likely there is a deep frustration or tension there. At some level he may be aware that he is not what he is pretending to be. He is a pretend lord of the manor, serving a pretend king. There is a mismatch between reality and his role. In trying to be what he is not, he is missing his true calling. Still, there is time to repent and begin again, there always is."

And he leant back contentedly.

"Well, that was a sermon indeed," said Will. "Let's remember that Gisborne has got more than I have. I am not feeling sorry for him yet."

"He has more little things than you have. But in the scales they are light compared to the weight of good friendships and a clear conscience. And perhaps he knows that."

"Robin, do not be down-hearted. You are still the Lord of the Manor," said Marian. "When it comes to fulfilling your calling, 'where' matters less than 'how'. You are still trying to look after your people."

"Perhaps, but I am not looking after them as well I would like, and I am not looking after the land," said Robin, and then, slightly ruefully, "and a comfortable bed and a solid roof have their attractions."

"I thought you were a soldier," said Marian. "Aren't you meant to enjoy all this sort of thing?"

"I sometimes enjoy it, usually simply survive it. And you are right, I am a soldier, I keep fighting the battle. But, old bones enjoy the hard ground less than they used to." He looked up. "Alan, we have had the Friar, let's have the minstrel. It is time to give us a song."

Alan Dale smiled: "What mood are you in?"

"I don't know," said Robin. "Perhaps that is the problem."

Alan took out his lute, and strummed it softly as he waited for the words to come. He then began.

You ask for a song
But do not say what style or tone or kind.
Do you need to laugh or need to cry?
What is truly on your mind?

You ask for a song
But do not say if you or me decide
What thoughts lie deep within you now
For the tune to lift or hide.

You ask for a song
And so I say that you should take the lead
Sing from the heart, sing from the soul
Sing clear, sing strong, sing free.

"The song I would sing," said Robin, "is a mix of slow and fast, sad and happy. I am here with my friends and I am alive. But I am sad that I have lost my home and am not serving my people as best I can." He looked up at Tuck. "Does my talkative Friar have anything to add?"

"You are not the first and you won't be the last to suffer injustice," Tuck replied. "Do you remember that evening as we watched the sunset over Jerusalem, when you heard this poem?"

I wonder how love feels
when it seems to lose and die
but knows the deep and ancient truth
that all will be put right.

I wonder how it hurt
as the Judas kiss came close
and affection died away
in the face of your old friend.

I wonder how it hurt
as the soldiers threw you down
before those fragile men,
dressed up in worldly power.

I wonder how it hurt
as Pilate turned away
and washed his hands of wanting
to stand for truth and life.

I wonder how it hurt
as nails were hammered in
and blood from cruel thorns
was drying on your face.

I wonder how love feels
when it seems to lose and die
but knows the deep and ancient truth
that all will be put right.

"I remember, Friar, I remember Jerusalem," said Robin. "But I do not think we can apply those words to me. All I have lost is some walls and a roof. Let's not get carried away."

Tuck smiled. "All suffering counts, all suffering matters. Some suffering is even holy. But you are right, it is good to keep some perspective."

Chapter 7

An Archery Contest

A boy raised his hand.

"Sorry, Miss, change of topic: Didn't Robin Hood steal from the rich to give to the poor? Can he really be a hero?"

"Thank you," said Emma. "That is a good question, let me see what I can do." She thought for a moment and then continued:

After a pause, Will Scathlock looked up: " 'All will be put right', you said, Friar. Perhaps so, perhaps so, Friar, but our own particular hero for justice—" and he rolled his eyes affectionately, "is known to be stealing from the rich, albeit to give to the poor. Is that quite the example of saintly reputation you have in mind?"

Tuck smiled. "This is part of what our particular leader feels he needs to do for the sake of others. But it is not really about money. Think what Gisborne has: Status, recognition, security. Robin wants the poor to have these, as well. He wants them to know that they are as valued as the Lord in the castle. And so here in the forest each person has a role, each person has a title, and Robin doesn't even have to take anything from Gisborne to give it to them. But if they need food as well as honour, then some of Gisborne's money comes in useful. Gisborne still has enough, and he took the money from the villagers in the first place. He can still possess what he thinks he has, but there will come a time when he realises that the titles and dressing up mean nothing compared with how he feels inside."

"But it can still be argued that Robin is taking."

"These things did not truly belong to Gisborne. Robin is restoring, not stealing."

"Does that not mean he is simply setting himself up as judge?"

"It would be if he were acting on his own behalf, but constantly in his mind is what the true king would want."

"King Richard is not perfect."

"None of our leaders are, but we have to use what reference points we can."

Will smiled, "I think there may be some special pleading going on."

"Perhaps. But an old Friar has to do his best."

"And I am keeping well out of the discussion," said Robin. "I am a simple soldier, and if people are hungry I will feed them. And if the rich need help to travel more lightly, I will help them to do so. And sometimes I will make wrong decisions. But I think, I hope, I am wanting the right outcomes. Does that make a difference?"

At that moment John Forrest came striding into the glade. "More news," he said. "And we might have some fun with this. There are notices all through the county: there is to be an archery contest tomorrow for the sheriff's birthday. The prize is a silver arrow."

"If Robin won he would lose it like he loses all his other arrows. Wasted on him, I'll have to do it," said Will Scathlock

"We could take Tuck and he could bore them to sleep with his sermons while we steal the arrow?" said John Forrest.

"Thank you for your usual encouragement and wisdom!" said Robin. "But I think this one is for me."

"It is likely to be a trap," said Marian.

"I agree, but I will still go as I am, not in disguise. Our band has grown larger than Gisborne suspects. We will fight our way out of the trap if we need. It would cheer the villagers if I won, and they would notice if I stayed away. I think it is worth the risk."

"Do you think they regret forcing you out?"

"Probably not, my presence was becoming dangerous for them. It was the right decision. But perhaps some are sad that it had to be done."

***

Guy of Gisborne smiled when he saw Robin emerge from the forest and walk on to the archery field. "The man in the hood returns," he said to himself, and then quietly to his guards: "When I give the sign, seize him. Whatever happens, seize him. Whatever he says, seize him. Whatever he does, seize him. Whatever the crowd does, seize him. Am I clear?"

His guards nodded.

The contest began. Sixteen archers took part, after each round the targets were placed three yards further away. One by one the contestants fell out. And then there were two left, Robin Locksley and a man from the village called Smith Smithson.

Gisborne rose from his cushioned chair that had been carried to the field and placed under a purple canopy. "The contestants will pause," he announced, "and spectators can move closer if they wish." He gestured to his guards to step forward; they stood ready, either side of him.

The two remaining contestants sat down on the grass.

"Master Smithson," said Robin. "How much do you want to win this?" Smith gestured over to the side of the field, two children were watching: "This is for them. It has been a hard winter."

"This will make them proud of you?"

"Master Locksley, we have both noticed Gisborne's guards, we do not know how this day will end. So, may I speak plainly? I have little book-learning, but I am known as an honest smith and I say it as I see it. I think as I work, I listen when others talk and I watch when others act."

Robin nodded. "You have as much right to speak as I do, or as anyone does."

"Then let me say this. If I think I can win my children's pride or love by notching up archery victories, I am not understanding them. They were born wanting to love their parents. That is what children do, all of them. That says nothing special about me or what I can do, it is how they are. All I have to do is try and care for them as best I can. They will forgive mistakes, they will understand my failings, they will want to cheer me on, whatever I do. Whether I lose or win, they will feel the same. Parents who disappoint their children do so in rather different ways than by losing archery competitions. Those who disappoint are those who deliberately stop being on their children's side, who get too fixed on other targets, and it is this that

confuses and upsets a child."

Robin gazed thoughtfully. "You are blessed with wisdom Master Smithson, and I am guessing there are stories behind what you say. I would wish for more of your conversation." He glanced across at the children, and then across to where Marian, Alan, John, Tuck and Will were standing. "We need wisdom in these times."

"In all times."

"Smithson will shoot first," cried Gisborne.

They stood up.

Smith Smithson turned to face the target and took up his stance.

His arrow thudded into the edge of the inner circle.

Robin's did the same.

Smith's next one was a few inches further out.

There was stillness as Robin drew his bow back. He released; the arrow flew straight but not quite true. It hit midway between the circle and the outer edge of the target. He turned to Smithson: "You have won. Well done, well done."

And he turned to the watching children and called out: "Your father is a fine archer, but, much more than that, he is a fine father."

He turned back and saw Gisborne's soldiers running toward him. He stood still and fitted an arrow to his bow.

"Stop!" he commanded, and such was the authority in his

voice that they stopped, or perhaps it was the realisation that if they continued at least one of them would fall.

"Look to your right."

And they did, and saw three bows similarly aimed directly at them. And, leaving Alan, Marian and Will in their positions, John Forrest was striding across the grass, carrying his great oak staff. Tuck joined him, almost running to keep up.

Gisborne's voice was then heard, almost a scream, "Seize Locksley, you cowards."

Smith Smithson stepped forward.

He raised his bow.

"No. This man lives. Villagers, to me."

And before anyone knew what was happening the villagers were running towards Smith. They crowded round him and Robin. The two men glanced at each other and began walking towards where Gisborne sat. The guards fell back as the throng advanced, and surrounded their master defensively, swords at the ready. The villagers halted.

There was a commotion and some murmurings in the crowd but Tuck was good with his elbows and made his way through. He reached the front, turned and faced the villagers. He raised a hand and they fell silent; he turned back to face Guy of Gisborne: "You have tried to rule by fear. That works for a time but only a time. Fear will never gain loyalty or affection. There will come a day when people will stop being afraid and then you will find that you have no relationship, no authority. Your role will end."

"My authority comes from the king," said Guy.

"It does not come from the true king, it comes from a false imposter. Your pride and your trust must not rest in him. Gisborne it is time to go."

"You forget, stupid little Friar, that my guards are here. And within a day other soldiers will join me."

Tuck turned to the guards.

"He rules you with contempt as well. It is time for you to come from fear to freedom. Serve Locksley, not Gisborne. Serve the true Lord of the Manor. Make the right choice. Make it now."

And then the bell went.

Emma looked at the pupils. "Well, if you were Gisborne's guards, what would you do?"

Chapter 8

The Courage of Annabel

Annabel made her way to room 868 at lunchtime, and there she saw Miss Loss, Mr Ladd and a man she did not know.

"I was looking for Miss Armstrong and thought she might be here," she said, standing slightly awkwardly in the doorway. "I want to tell her that my friends and I have been talking, and if we had been the guards we would have joined Robin Hood."

Jenny smiled. "Hello, Annabel, thank you. We will pass your message on."

"Annabel, I do not think we have met," said the man. "My name is Mr Vincent." And he stepped forward and shook her hand. "I am a Governor of the school and I sometimes call in to see how things are going. I do not know exactly what stories Miss Armstrong has been telling you. But may I say that I think you have made a very good choice, it is always wise to choose to join Robin Hood." He turned to Gary. "What does our musician in residence have to say?"

Gary smiled. "Annabel, it is good to see you again; Mr Vincent, is this your way of asking for a song?"

"Well, I think it is. You being here, this being this room, Annabel beginning this journey. It all seems to fit. Annabel, you better come and sit down as well, who knows how long Mr Ladd will take to think of something?"

Annabel stepped into the room. She was still a little nervous, but she sat down, near Miss Loss whom she knew the best. She had not been in this room before and she did not quite know why she thought it would be right to look here for Miss Armstrong.

Gary replied: "I don't think I can do a song right now. But I look at you, Annabel, and I want simply to affirm your courage. It takes courage to come up the stairs to look for Miss Armstrong and to walk into a room of teachers. It takes courage to think that if you were a guard you would have left Guy of Gisborne and gone into an uncertain chapter with Robin Hood and Maid Marian and the others. It takes courage to think deeply about what song you want to sing."

"Why do you think you would have joined Robin Hood?" asked Jenny.

Annabel said thoughtfully, "Perhaps I want to leave Guy of Gisborne behind because I can't cope with any more pressure. Life is busy at the moment and I am feeling under so much pressure from so many things. Work, home, friends, expectations, all the normal things. And that's what he represents: pressure, doesn't he? All those weekly targets and demands. But he also represents familiarity? That is why it is a difficult choice. I know what the pressures are; perhaps I don't want to break free from what I know."

She noticed the adults glance at each other. Jenny said, "Annabel, I think we are all thinking the same, that you are a remarkably perceptive and wise person. Mr Ladd has rightly affirmed your courage. As a teacher, I simply want to say: 'Well done for thinking so clearly and knowing yourself so well.'"

Jenny continued: "These old stories, like Robin Hood,

have lasted so long and been so popular because they touch themes that have echoes in all of us. It is wise to ask your friends how they cope, and it is equally wise to ask people from centuries ago, reading the histories and stories of those who kept going even when things were difficult. No situation is the same, no pressures are identical, but we can still learn lessons.

"May I give you eight suggestions that summarise some of the old wisdom? Sleep well, look after yourself physically, look after your friendships, keep things in perspective, think about the balance between work and leisure, be thankful at the end of each day, stay focused on helping other people, and if faith matters to you, hold on to it."

"That all sounds rather too easy," said Annabel.

"Something can sound simple to do but be quite difficult to put into practice. How determined are you? Try imagining a day which includes some or all of these eight. Part of the challenge, when handling pressure, is discovering the right way of strengthening the person's determination to find the right rhythm for the day, the right rhythm for the week." Jenny paused. "Do you feel you have the determination? It is sometimes difficult, as you said, to break free from the patterns imposed by those such as Guy of Gisborne."

Annabel shook her head slowly. "I need time to think of all this, and you will need to write down those eight points for me to remember."

Mr Vincent leant forward: "May I add something? It fits in with what Mr Ladd said about courage. Part of whether we can cope or not is whether we have the courage to keep going. Whatever the stress, whatever the pressure, do we have the courage to keep going, to do the right thing, to see something through, day by day?

"Let me tell you a story from the old days. I have to admit (and here he hesitated and Jenny smiled at his unwonted self-consciousness), it involved me:

We were sitting at the Round Table. Gawain was not there, I think that was the time when he was dealing with the Green Knight. Lamorak was somewhere, I can't remember now. Arthur looked round and said: "Someone must deal with the magician hiding in the woods. I hear tales that some sheep nearby are scared by his late-night wanderings and spell-practising."

There were not many volunteers. I agreed to go.

I heard the encouragement and cheering as I left; this happens for any knight who leaves for a quest. But as soon as I left the warmth of Camelot I felt heavy-hearted. The weather was cold, cheerless and wet. I thought I was riding quickly but the road seemed to lengthen in front of me and time seemed to slow down. I wondered why I had agreed to go, this was not a glamourous quest. No dragons, no tournaments, no rescues. No one would be singing songs about this one, this little quest to calm down an old man who sometimes got rather carried away. Days passed. I wondered what they were all doing in Camelot and why I couldn't have stayed and been with them. The strange thing was that I had been on many quests, but they had never bothered me like this one. The clouds were heavy and the road was muddy. My best blue coat had fallen off. Had I lost my way? Had I missed the right part of the forest? I had decided to turn round when I caught a memory in my mind of Arthur saying "Who will go?" and his face when he asked it. So I kept going.

My horse went lame. I slowed to a walk and stopped at a hut. The peasant living there agreed to look after the horse until I returned. I did not know if I could trust him or not but felt I had no choice.

"Why don't you go back to Camelot?" he asked.

"This is my path, I must stick to it."

"Back at Camelot they must think you are foolish giving your time to this."

Perhaps they did, but then I remembered that this was not how they were. The true knights do not think others are foolish if their motives are in place.

And so I continued on, step by step, and then at last I was at the outskirts of the wood. I could not see the way in. There seemed to be no path and so I began to clamber over fallen trees and force my way through bushes. It felt pointless, but I went on.

And I reached a clearing, and there was a cottage the other side. I walked across, now drawing myself up to my full height, walking as Lancelot, the king's champion, should walk. A little old man came out.

"Lancelot," he said. "You have won, I lay down my powers, I will now serve Arthur of Camelot."

I stopped and looked at him, fearing some kind of trap.

"You have conquered because each time you wished to turn back, you did not. You showed courage. Some can show the hot desperate courage of fighting dragons or giants when they suddenly appear on the path ahead; you showed courage in the face of tiredness, loneliness, pointlessness and despair. The heaviness was caused by my magic, but your courage to keep going broke the spell. Each time you decided to take another step, my spell was weakened a little more, and now it is nothing."

He then looked at me thoughtfully.

"Perhaps you needed to come on this quest for your sake as well as for mine."

Mr Vincent looked at Annabel. "Be courageous, be committed to do what is right and keep on doing it. Always."

Annabel replied: "You said that the story involved you. But that was about King Arthur and his knights, although I don't know much about all that. Why did you say you were in the story? Were you pretending to be the Lancelot one?"

"We could say I was pretending," said Mr Vincent. "But it is not quite the right word."

"I will write down for you the eight points about handling pressure," said Jenny

"And I will tell Miss Armstrong about the choice you made," said Gary. "She will be very grateful you listened so well to the story. I have now thought of a poem, I am sorry it is not a song. Would you like to hear it?"

"Yes please," said Annabel. So Gary began:

The devil called a meeting – a kind of training day –
Setting out the game plan, for tempters to obey.
"Humanity's the target. Emptiness we sell.
Come on boys let's at 'em – Let's really give them hell!

Keep them busy, keep them at it. Keep them occupied.
Never give them time to ask if they are satisfied.

Let them trust in idols, created in their minds,
Not crude and wooden statues, but deeper, subtler kinds
– 'How do I look? Do I succeed? Do people notice me?
Am I tall and rich and bright, and perfect as should be?'

Keep them stressed out, keep them wound up, keep them petrified.
Never give them time to ask if they are satisfied.

Keep them from good pleasure, from wanting to be free.
From seeing the potential of all that they can be.
From friendships, fun and laughter, from joy at each new day.
From searching for the purer light, that drives our lies away."

There was a pause.

"Thank you," said Annabel, "and thank you, everyone. I better go now, I have a lesson soon." She left the room and went downstairs. There was so much to think about. Downstairs in the corridor she bumped into Emma.

"Hello, Annabel," Emma said.

"Hello, Miss. I am enjoying the stories. Thank you for them. I hope the guards chose Robin Hood."

She then looked directly at Emma. "Miss, what is going on?"

Chapter 9

Staying Patient, Staying Thankful

The next afternoon Mark Lind was sitting with Rex English at a table in the café. He said: "I know this should not trouble me, but I really do not seem to have much of a role this time."

"As I said before, your calling is to wait well. And, Mark, that can indeed be so difficult. But perhaps it can be liberating to know that things can happen without you? If at other times you feel fully involved, remember then that the significance of your part may be less than you think. Such things cannot be easily measured and we never accurately see the effects of what we do. But can't you see, at the very least, your part in helping Emma to be a storyteller and poet was and is a rich gift? Is that not enough?"

At the same time Gary, Emma and Jenny were sitting in room 868.

"How is it going?" Jenny asked Emma.

"I am about halfway though. I am enjoying being here, but am not quite sure what use I am."

"Who knows what effect your stories may be having? But I happen to know that the Headmaster is now as concerned about you as he is about Gary. And that is good news. He may almost have forgotten that he is here." Jenny looked at her watch. "If you are both free now, can you come to the café with me?"

They walked separately through different corridors and

down different staircases so they would not be seen together as they left the school.

When they arrived at the café, Rex English and Mark stood to greet them and Mr English said: "The owner of the café is a friend of mine and there is a room upstairs we can use. Follow me."

And he led them to a door next to the kitchen and they slipped through, and then up a narrow staircase. Along a short dark corridor and Mr English opened another door. In the small, wood-panelled room there was a round table. Sitting there was Mr Vincent, he stood courteously when the others came in. Mr English gestured to them all to find places without ceremony.

"This is a brief meeting to say thank you to each one for the part you have played so far in this chapter."

"Not much seems to have happened," said Emma.

"A great deal has happened and there is much to be thankful for," said Rex English. "And when it is hard to see what there is to be thankful for, then we simply work a little harder to see it.

"So let me begin with you, dear Emma. You have seized the opportunity and told stories well. And Mr Aldwyn has felt happy that his lessons now seem calmer and more popular than ever, and something has been re-awoken in him, which will make a difference to generations of pupils to come.

"Jenny is still in post, that in itself is significant, considering all that she stands for. Gary is still at the school. And his quest is beyond all our thinking. As long as he is still standing, then there is much to be thankful for. Mr Vincent is still a Governor. Mark is learning the virtue of apparently being unimportant. So thank you all for what you are doing."

"I am starting to realise that it is difficult to know how large the twinkle is in your eye when you speak," said Emma.

"I smile a lot," said Rex English. "Sometimes it shows on the outside."

"Give us a story, Mark, or a poem, or both," said Jenny. "Make a difference to us this afternoon, sitting here at this table, right now."

Emma said: "How about a Sir Richard one, like you used to do."

After a brief explanation to Mr Vincent about Sir Richard, the honourable knight who long ago fought in peace and war to defend the freedom of his people, Mark began:

Sir Richard sat quietly. His beloved Catherine had died some years before. He was old and ill. He got cold easily and sat for long periods in this small room in his castle, wrapped in a blanket, out of the drafts and the space of the big hall. draughts

There was a knock on the door. It was a servant, asking him to come down to the hall; some people were there to see him. Richard got up slowly and followed his servant. In the hall he stood, supporting himself by resting his hands on the top of a chair. Near the big doors leading to the courtyard there was a child, the daughter of one of his villagers. She came over to him and held out an egg. "My mother told me to bring you an egg," she said, quickly. "This egg is from a duck. This duck was from an egg from a duck that was from an egg from a duck (here the little girl looked a little flustered) that came from an egg from a

65

duck. Anyway, lots and lots of ducks that go back to when my father first had his land and pond given back after you got rid of Sir Adam. My mother wants you to know that she is still grateful, and that the ducks are still laying eggs."

"Thank you for the egg," said Sir Richard, and he smiled. The little girl bowed and turned and left.

A young man stepped forward. He held a wooden stool. "This is the first thing I have made," he said. "My father said that it was you who gave him his first carpentry tools when he was young. He was very poor then, and from those tools he built up his livelihood."

"I remember your father well, he was a good man. I had forgotten about the tools. I am glad they have been useful." The young man smiled, and left.

A couple walked over to him, holding a baby. "This is our little girl, Mary," the mother said. "We were only able to get married because you brought peace and safety to our village. We wanted you to see the baby."

"Thank you," said Sir Richard. He smiled at the baby and the couple. "May Mary grow to bring peace and safety to others. She is blessed to have you as parents."

The little family left.

The hall was now empty of visitors. But Richard stayed standing where he was, still steadying himself on the chair and gazed round at this space that had seen so much. He tried to recall faces and events, feelings and moments. So many faces, many only half-remembered but still golden in his mind as the afternoon sun lit up the hall through the high windows. He smiled slightly. An egg, a stool, a child. Perhaps he should be more thankful for what he had been part of. Perhaps he should make more of an effort to remember. There was a poignancy in it all, as well. Was he able still to do something for anyone? Or were those days now past?

Gary said quietly: "The Grail reminds us that there is no past. Or present or future. Whatever is true, is. Whatever was done in love, is. The gifts are always being given, are always being received."

"Yesterday," said Emma, "a pupil named Annabel, whom some of you have met, asked what was going on. What should I say?"

"Is she right for the Table?" asked Mr Vincent. "It seems to me that she is. At the moment we are only six."

"Seven is always better," Mr English nodded. "However, it is the right people more than the right number that counts. But I agree, Annabel sounds a very positive addition. Let us pause for a moment and I will meet her. In the meantime, Emma, tell her the truth. Whatever you understand to be going on, tell her.

"Thank you everyone for being here this afternoon. Continued thanks for all you do. We will see how the week unfolds."

And the meeting finished.

***

Three days later Mark Lind and Emma Armstrong met after school in the café; this time they were downstairs, as normal.

"Have you enjoyed the time at school?" Mark was asking.

"Yes," said Emma. "But I don't want to talk about that

now. I want to ask about Jenny Loss and Mr Vincent. If I have got my Arthur stories right, then Guinevere and Lancelot got things badly wrong. But here they are, as part of the Table as ever. Why don't they have those same voices telling them they are not good enough that I continue to have, the ones I mentioned in the poem?"

"I cannot be quite sure," said Mark, "and remember that I don't know much more than you do about the stories, nor about these two; we never quite know what is going on inside other people, anyway. But what I would guess is this: they have talked through honestly whatever needed to be talked through, that always helps. Secondly, I think they allow themselves to hear the positive voices as well as the negative. Perhaps they consciously seek out the wholesome and forgiving voices and so the destructive ones don't have so much of a foothold. And whenever there is attention to the Grail, there will be an emphasis on restoration and forgiveness. We are all part of Gary's quest."

Emma stared at the table. "I think I need something comforting and reassuring. How about a story about the little boy who liked the candles?"

"That was a long time ago. I will try. But it won't of course be very good."

Emma threw the paper napkin at him. "Just have a go. If I sometimes have to be Merlin, then so do you."

Mark smiled. "A fair point. Here it is."

It was the morning of Tommy's birthday. Last year he had enjoyed a special day, the front room of the house had been lit up by a candle made by a kind old candle-maker. The candle had been full of light and colours and scents and had made the whole house feel warm. He wondered what would happen this year; the candle-maker had moved away.

He was sitting in the front room with his mother. She did not have much money but he knew she would do what she could. And her kindness and her time were more important than any number of expensive toys. They played games and talked. The day drew on, the autumn light began to fade and the street lamps began to glow. Tommy asked if he should draw the curtains and was just getting up to do so when there was a knock on the door.

A delivery man was there and he had two parcels. Both addressed to Tommy.

The first one had one or two rather ugly things.

The second was crammed full of beautiful objects.

The second had been sent by a very kind neighbour.

The first by someone who did not think very much of him at all.

"My extra present for your birthday," said his mother, "is this: I promise to remind you, every day, that the second box matters more than the first. You may need occasionally to face up to what is in the first box, you may need to deal with what is ugly and painful. But remember that you do that best when you remember that you have the second box, and who gave it to you."

Tommy looked up. "Thank you," he said, "I think I will play with the second box now."

Emma reached over and took his hand. "Thank you, Mark, for reminding me about the good box." She then said, in a more matter-of-fact voice: "Arthur told me to ask you for a story, and so I did. And then I was to give you this." She handed him an envelope.

He took the envelope, opened it and drew out a single small piece of paper. Written on it was this: "Mark, the waiting is over; it is time for you to go to Glastonbury."

Chapter 10

Glastonbury

The next day, in his office, Ed Moore was speaking to an unwelcome but not unexpected visitor: "I am not sure why I should work for you anymore."

"I have got you to where you are; you are on the winning side and let's not throw things away now," replied Morgan Le Fay. "Don't you see that these feeble old ideas are disappearing? You are being affected by these silly little stories. Stay with me, Ed, there is a great future ahead."

There was a knock at the door.

"Yes?" both men replied.

The secretary opened the door; she looked at them and settled on Mr Moore to address: "I am sorry to interrupt, Sir," she said. "Mr Ladd has just called. He gave me a message for you. He is wondering if now is the right time for him to go to Glastonbury." She withdrew.

The two men looked at each other. Le Fay said: "If that thing is brought back here who knows what will happen. We must move quickly. Stop him leaving the school."

They turned to the door, but it opened before they reached it and there stood Mr Vincent.

"Ah, I am so sorry, Mr Vincent," said Mr Moore. "I was not expecting you and, as you can see, I am just going out."

"Not yet," said Lancelot, with a smile.

"I am afraid I really must, right now. I need to see a member of staff immediately about a matter of great importance."

"You want to, but you don't need to," Mr Vincent said. "In fact, it could be argued that what you need is for him to go, and for you not to stop him."

"You may be a Governor but you have no right to be listening at the door," said Mr Le Fay.

"I was not listening. I happen to know what is happening and I know how both your minds work. And, Le Fay, you are not a Governor and have no right to be here at all."

"He is my guest," said Ed.

"Oh, I thought he was your master."

Mr Moore took a step forward. "I am a busy man, Mr Vincent, I am leaving my study now, please move aside."

"No."

Ed Moore and Morgan Le Fay looked at each other. Mr Vincent smiled at them both.

"Interesting, isn't it," said Mr Vincent, "that with all your plans and technologies you cannot cope with the simple strategy of someone standing in the doorway. You are feeling out of your comfort zone, but that is because you have made your comfort zone so small. A thousand of my adversaries from the old days would have known what to do, but you do not. Let me present you with the choices that fit who you are, and help you decide. You can shout for help but if any help comes, the resulting struggle will use up precious minutes and you may not win, I am not sure there is anyone on this site with my experience of winning such encounters. You can call the police, that would take even more minutes and the publicity would not be good. You can rush me yourselves, but you would not succeed and I do not recommend that you try. Or, you can wait for five minutes, and I will then allow you to go. If I were you, that is the option I would choose."

The two men looked at each other, and then at Mr Vincent, standing nonchalantly in the doorway. Le Fay shrugged and looked at the floor, occasionally looking at his watch.

After five minutes Mr Vincent stepped aside. He watched the two men run through the door, ignoring the receptionist, race down the corridor and towards the car park. *Enjoy the drive*, he said to himself, and smiled.

***

Classroom 868 was full of people. *This brings back memories*, thought Jenny Loss, as she looked at the faces, lit by a single candle burning on the desk. This time Rex English was not there, nor Mark Lind. But Emma Armstrong and Gary Ladd were, as they had been as children all those years ago. Annabel was there. Jenny looked up as Lancelot came in. He walked over and whispered: "I held them long enough so that when they left they would be so impatient that they would not check he had actually gone. To move without thinking, that is what we wanted them to do. And they did. Well, I have had some tasks in my time, but this is the first time I have stood in a doorway so that the dragons ran the wrong way."

He smiled and fell silent, and found a place to sit. Jenny nodded to Gary. He moved to behind the desk, sat down and began to speak: "I have been thinking about the Grail, ever since, or perhaps just before, I asked for a poem about it in a lesson in this school many years ago. It was then in

73

this very room I heard the poem itself.

Did the hands that shape the cup know the meaning it would hold?
Or see the deepening stories that unendingly unfold?
The wine, the blood, the vision, the quest across the sea
The strange and flowing riches that fashioned Glastonbury.

Did the hands that share the cup know the searching it would bring
From knights and nameless pilgrims who wished to serve their king?
Did they sense the drawing power of all that lay within,
The fellowship, the sacrifice, of losing all to win?

"There have been times when I stopped searching, when I was distracted or lazy, but I think the underlying desire was always somewhere there. In the searching, I have learnt the truth of Mr English's words: it is not the Grail that matters, it is what it points to.

"The Grail points to ultimate goodness, and those who truly seek find themselves changed as they search. If we look for something that speaks of love, hospitality, forgiveness, liberation, sacrifice, victory and joy, then these qualities shape us as we travel, they begin to become part of who we are. In becoming part of who we are, they then become part of what we share with others.

"The old stories had it that Galahad achieved perfection and thus could find the Grail. If that is so, then our understanding of perfection needs to change. I am not perfect at all, but I am at peace, because I am forgiven. If forgiveness is one of the themes of this quest then I must accept that I have need of being forgiven. I am vulnerable and needy, but I do not fret, because I know I belong. The joy of this feast is not that I deserve it or earn it, but that I am invited to receive and share it, as I am. The joy of this feast is that others are freely invited, we gather together round the table.

"So this is my call to arms to you. I want you to seek the things of the Grail, not the things of this world. And

74

whenever you see behaviour that speaks of selfishness, cruelty, a lust for gold, status, fame, or control, then speak out against it. Protect your friends from being tainted, protect the weak from being trampled.

"And keep watch on yourselves. The battle starts within us."

***

Two hours later Ed Moore and Morgan Le Fay stood at the west end of the ruins of Glastonbury Abbey and looked down its length.

"Why here?" said Ed.

"Because the legend has it that Joseph of Arimathea brought the cup here. And that monks found the tomb of King Arthur here. It would be a natural place for Ladd to look. But I cannot see him, perhaps we overtook him on the way."

There was a movement to one side of them and a figure emerged from the shadow cast by the ancient stones. But it was not Gary Ladd, it was Mark Lind.

"You did not overtake him because you were not on the same road," said Mark, "and probably never have been, but that is another story." He smiled. "By the way, it is rather unlikely that King Arthur is really buried here. We cannot be absolutely certain about the Joseph story, but that seems very unlikely, too. Good evening, Mr Moore. It seems a long time since you arranged my dismissal from St. George's. And your companion must be your master Morgan Le Fay?"

Ed Moore flushed with anger, but as he did so he knew that it was the use of the word 'master' that annoyed him most. "What is all this about?" he asked.

Morgan Le Fay asked: "Where is Gary Ladd?"

"Oh, he decided not to come. Remember, the message only said that he was wondering about going to Glastonbury; he did not say he was going to. But you jumped to a conclusion. You thought you were running out of time and you rushed. You did not check. Mr Vincent played his part well."

"So he is no longer interested in the Grail?" queried Le Fay.

"As interested as ever. But he does not need at the moment to see or touch it. His quest led him to stay where he was this afternoon."

"So he is still at school?" said Ed Moore.

"What you say implies that the Grail is actually here, and Ladd simply is being patient. You know it's here, don't you?" interrupted Morgan Le Fay.

"Yes, it is here. But you will not find it. Would you like one of my poems, Ed, just like the old days?"

"No."

And then Ed Moore asked again: "So he is still at school?"

"Yes," said Mark. "There are things he needed to say there. If you do not want to hear more from me, I will go." Mark Lind bowed slightly and slipped back behind the base of the ruined arch.

Ed Moore turned to Le Fay: "What do we do?"

"We grab Lind and make him tell us where that stupid cup is, or we dig this place up until we find it ourselves."

They looked round, but there was now no sign of Mark.

"This place is huge," said Ed. "It could be anywhere, and I feel that this earth has seen too much, both good and evil, over the centuries. There is life and peace here but there is death and sorrow. Whatever lies underneath should be left there. I don't want to disturb it any more. Anyway, I thought you didn't believe in all this. Let's go."

"Why do you think I should take any notice of what you say?" said Le Fay. "You forget who I am. And how come you are becoming sentimental about a patch of grass and some old ruins? You forget that we deal in reality, in what we can see and touch, in what is here now. And we need the cup. Of course I don't believe all that rubbish surrounding it, but fools like Gary Ladd and Mark Lind do, and their mistaken passion annoys me and could yet affect what we are trying to do. When I find it, I'll destroy it. Utterly."

Ed Moore looked again at the peaceful site, the grass stretching to the old kitchen, the path leading to the thorn bush. The old stones that had survived theft, lies and dissolution. He remembered how the Abbot of Glastonbury had been taken and hung at the top of the nearby hill. He felt the depth of the past. He was unused to such feelings. He turned and walked away.

Outside the gate he paused.

"How did you get here?" The voice was that of Mark Lind.

"In Le Fay's car."

"Let's leave it for him. I'll take you back."

77

Ed Moore nodded and walked with Mark towards his car. He stopped abruptly and said: "Lind, what's happening to me?"

"I don't know."

"Then I will push you to think. Talk to me about friendship. Your group has a loyalty and respect that clearly matters. What makes it work?"

"There is something about commitment to a common cause, although I admit I am not always sure what the cause is. I do not know all that is in Arthur's mind, but I know him well enough to trust that he is worth following, and worth obeying if he asks me to take on a task. There is an understanding that each of us will do all we can to help each other in whatever we, individually or together, are called to do. And I think there is enjoyment in our differences, we don't want to be all the same or have the same views. We work hard at the including and the belonging. Why do you ask?"

"Because I cannot tell if Le Fay is on my side or not. I don't think he is interested in me at all, only what I can contribute to his plans. And I am wondering why I did not notice all this earlier."

"It is always flattering to think we are needed. Slightly less so if we are made to realise that it is not us in ourselves that matter to the other person, but only something we can bring. If the friendship is real he will want the best for you. What use you may be for him will always be secondary."

"I am wondering why all this is coming clearer now."

"As if the mist is lifting? Perhaps there is something here about what you went to Glastonbury to find."

Ed Moore looked up sharply. He turned back to the ruined abbey and gazed across the grass and stones.

"I think I can manage one of your poems now," he said.

"Here it is," said Mark.

There are days when the door is nudged
Just ajar
And the light slants in
Or glints in the cracks between the hinges.

There are days when the door is opened
Wide and full
And the light floods in
Almost blinding, overwhelming.

There are days when the door is closed
And the light is held
At a distance, forgotten,
Until the next time.

"Was that it?" said Ed

"That's it," said Mark. He shrugged apologetically. "Let's drive now. School is waiting."

Chapter 11

The Wolves Are Coming Near

When Mark Lind and Ed Moore arrived back in school one or two pupils saw the car and waved cheerfully at their Headmaster.

Ed Moore smiled and returned the waves. This felt a new beginning, there was something friendly in the air. He got out of the car and walked purposefully to his study. There he half-expected to see someone waiting to greet him, to welcome him, to tell him all was well. But his room was empty. Nothing had changed.

But he felt as if something had. But he did not know what it was. Or what it might mean.

There was a knock on the door. His secretary pushed the door open: "Mr Le Fay is here, Sir, as arranged."

Not by me, Ed wanted to say. He looked at the door and Morgan Le Fay walked in.

"Sit, sit, my friend," said Le Fay expansively, and Ed realised he had not heard this tone before. They sat.

"I can travel quickly when need be," said Le Fay. He gave a self-deprecatory smile. "No doubt Mr Lind's driving feels more comfortable than mine. And I know his tricks, a little bit of atmosphere, a poem or two, some soft words? They play as manipulatively as we do and have no scruples. But – and here is the big 'but', Ed, – does his thinking match up to mine? He deals in stories, the dead past, poems and feelings. I deal in facts. What is he actually offering?"

"What do you mean by facts?" said Ed

"What I can see, touch, experience. What can be proved."

"You slipped in what you can experience, Mr Le Fay. I experienced the sunset yesterday as being beautiful. I believe that Duke William of Normandy won the Battle of Hastings but I cannot prove it in a laboratory. And I felt something at Glastonbury, I truly did. I wonder if your world is becoming a little too narrow for me."

"We all cope with our own crises in our own ways; I was hopeful that you would not be one of those ones who allow clear thinking to be muddled by smooth speech and a confusing day," said Mr Le Fay, and his voice became icier. "I am offering you a world of power. And power matters. Do you want to be on the winning side?"

"I don't think you know what victory really means."

Le Fay stood up, and suddenly Ed felt a profound fear, deeper than he had ever felt before. So deep he did not know what he was frightened of, but he sensed he was completely out of his depth. He felt very cold. Who was Le Fay? What could he do?

"If you are so keen on experience, don't ignore these feelings right now," said Le Fay. "One moment ago you were thinking about power and now you are very frightened, both feelings were caused by me and I can produce them whenever I wish. I can promise and I can threaten. Never forget what I can do, never forget what feelings I can spark, never forget what I am capable of."

He left.

Ed Moore remained sitting, his eyes closed. I could do with some normality after all that, he thought. He was almost relieved when the next knock on the door announced Gary Ladd.

Gary asked, "Sir, the pupils are very pleased to see you back. Would you like to speak to them? They are in the Hall."

Ed was an experienced enough Headteacher to know that this was a gentle but firm suggestion, not a question.

"Has someone arranged all of this? Of course, I will come now."

Standing in front of the pupils Mr Moore expressed gratitude for their welcome, commended them on their unity and purpose and told them they should go to the last lesson of the day. He nearly said something about what he had been through that day, he nearly told them about Glastonbury, but decided not to. He said nothing more.

The pupils dispersed to their classes and Emma found herself in front of the year group again.

Guy of Gisborne was to lead the attack himself. The forest was large but not impenetrable; for many weeks his scouts had searched for clues as to the whereabouts of Robin's camp. He had replaced the few guards who had deserted him at the archery tournament six months before; most had stayed with him and by paying for mercenaries he had increased his force. The words spoken by Tuck were easily ignored. Smithson would have to be dealt with, but he was popular in the village and as long as he stayed quiet there was no need to unsettle people by getting rid of him too soon.

Gisborne now felt he was strong enough to move directly against Robin. In the early days the outlaws had moved frequently, but as they became more settled, and as the group had become larger when others had joined them, they had increasingly stayed in one place, their original site in the glade in a heavily wooded side of a steep valley. It would take sharp eyes looking down a particular angle to see the camp and lookouts were always posted on the top of the ridge above. But thirty or forty people could not stay hidden for ever, and Gisborne knew roughly where the settlement was; one of Robin's band, returning from visiting a sick aunt, had been secretly followed.

The lookout that morning was Marian; Gisborne's men came quietly enough, but she could see occasional glimpses of sunlight reflecting off swords and she could sense the feel of many heavy feet across the forest floor. She knew that this force, approaching the ridge from the other side, preparing for an attack over the top, down into Robin's camp below, might be too large to resist.

She urgently found the other scouts and told them to return to the camp and warn the defenders. But she kept moving forward, down from the ridge, towards the intruders. And when Gisborne drew close she stepped out from behind her covering tree and stood before him. He stopped, and gestured for his men behind to stop.

"So, Marian, are you here to join us?"

"No, I am here to delay you. There is one path to the valley from this direction, I am standing in the way. You will have to fight me, perhaps kill me, to get past."

Gisborne dismounted, and stepped towards her. At that moment an arrow flew past him and struck Marian. The blow flung her back, her arms stretched wide and she fell.

Gisborne stared at the figure on the ground. He turned angrily around to his archers. "Stay where you are." He looked again at Marian. "What have I done?" he said *quietly.*

"Sir, surprise is vital, that is why she had to be dealt with quickly," said one of his archers, fitting another arrow to his bow. "Let's keep moving."

By this time one of the scouts had reached the clearing. Robin called to his closest friends and they drew away with the scout to the edge of the camp; they listened carefully to the news.

"They are many, and we have few weapons. And we are now looking after a large number of people, including children," said Alan Dale and he gestured to the families in the camp.

"We have some weapons, not many, but some," said Robin. "And we have many things that can be used as weapons. Whatever comes to hand, whatever can be held or thrown, whatever can be used to parry, we will use. We have what we have and it will be enough. We have the people who have joined us, and they will do what they can. Let us prepare."

Gisborne's men had speeded up. In half an hour they were at the top of the ridge itself and now started to stream down the slope towards the camp. But as they charged through the forest they were met with a bewildering defence. Children hid behind trees and simply pounded any passing foot or ankle with stones or sticks. It was not enough to stop a running knight but it distracted. Others threw any missile that came to hand. Women and men shouted and darted among the trees and when close enough might strike with a stout stick wrapped with brambles or a rusty cooking pan with edges jagged by age and use. Such improvised weapons had little direct effect except to slow down, annoy, and harass the attackers. With organisation, they could have easily have stood firm and swept away such irritations, but, they had been ordered to run fast towards the camp where they guessed Robin was; they had no time to regroup and reconsider. And at the same time they were facing the deadly fire from the hidden core of Robin's army. John, Alan, Will and Robin stayed out of sight but were firing with deadly accuracy. The attackers were caught in an ambush. One by one, one by one, Gisborne's men fell. The shouting and jeering and stones kept coming from all directions, and the swift, true arrows kept finding their mark. But there were still many left.

And then above all the noise there came the sound of the howl of a wolf. And then silence. The defenders scattered swiftly in different directions. And a voice called.

"Hasten, quickly, hasten. The wolves are coming near!"

Gisborne's men hesitated. And the voice came again.

"The people of the forest have gone. They know what the wolves can do. They have left the battle. If you wish to fight again, if you wish to live, then run, run back, run as you have never run before."

There was a great roar and John Forrest came into plain sight. He was wearing a heavy animal skin and seemed to have become larger than ever. He brandished his oak staff. "The wolves are coming near," he cried again. "Hasten, quickly, hasten!" And he strode towards Gisborne's knights. One, close to him, lunged with his sword; without breaking step John swung his staff and laid the knight out cold. He kept walking. "The wolves are with me. Run, run, if you want to live." The animal skin, the shouting, the sight of dead and wounded, the threat of the wolves, the silent arrows still flying, the man's great strength and fearlessness were enough. Gisborne shouted and cursed at his men, but their fear was too great. They turned and ran.

85

Over the ridge they went, and kept running.

Gisborne followed them and then stopped when he reached Marian's body, still lying on the path. He looked down for a moment.

"Guy, what have you done?"

Gisborne looked back and saw Friar Tuck walking up the path towards him.

Gisborne bent down and gently touched her face.

"Too much."

When he looked up again he saw that Tuck had been joined by John Forrest and Robin Locksley.

"Where are the wolves?" he asked.

"We are the wolves," said Robin. "Wolves are not always bad."

Gisborne stood up. "I will fight you. One to one. To settle this."

"No," said Tuck. "There has been enough death. And there is now the beginning of great grief. It is time, Guy, for you to go, away from here, away from the castle, away from this chapter of your life. It is time for you to go and to begin again."

Emma paused.

"Miss, is she dead?" a voice called out.

"She cannot have died, she is one of the heroes. She is only wounded," said another voice.

"Sometimes heroes die," said Emma.

And then the bell went.

Chapter 12

Taking a Seat at the Table

"It is beginning to swing our way," said Ed Moore. "A parent has complained that the stories being told by Emma Armstrong have upset their child. I'll tell old Aldwyn to get back in charge and Armstrong will have to go. She only had a few days left, anyway."

He was talking in his study to Morgan Le Fay. It was Monday morning, a new week. He felt rather ashamed of those strange feelings in Glastonbury and was pleased that he was getting back to his old self. He was back in charge.

Morgan Le Fay was all smiles. He explained to Ed Moore that a new and substantial honorarium was to be paid monthly to the Headmaster by his organisation. No need for anyone else to know. This was a purely private arrangement. They shook hands and Le Fay left to stroll around the grounds.

Later that day, Ed Moore was asked if he could see a pupil who had requested to talk to him. He was in expansive and relaxed mood, and agreed. Annabel came into the room. He ushered her to a seat and smiled warmly.

"Mr Aldwyn took our lesson again today," said Annabel. "He said Miss Armstrong had left. I am sad, Sir, that she had to leave."

"Ah, Annabel, yes, it is a shame. She was only meant to be here for a month, and sadly she had to leave before the end. Thank you so much for your concern."

"I heard that one parent had complained. If that is true,

then that is unfair on the rest of us."

"I understand it was a very, very upsetting story. And of course I cannot comment on a possible communication from any parent. Thank you, Annabel; I think that is all I can say on this matter."

"None of us were upset, a bit sad, of course, but we know what stories are like. We know that people die, sometimes in real life, as well as in stories. It was Flo's dad, wasn't it? Well, Flo was fine about the story, but her dad does tend to want to take control and impose his views on pretty much everything that happens. He likes to make a fuss, whether or not Flo wants him to."

"I cannot possibly comment. Thank you for your thoughts, Annabel, but my mind is made up."

"It is strange how people can't cope with stories they don't want to hear."

Ed Moore said sharply, "That is enough, Annabel. I think I must end this conversation now. It is time for you to go."

Annabel shrugged her shoulders and left.

When she was gone the Headmaster went back to his desk. His mood had changed and the lightness had gone. He was cross with Annabel for disturbing his re-found good humour. He grabbed some papers and looked carefully through them, hurriedly marking any point that may be of some interest, but he knew that he was not to be so easily distracted. It was ironic, he thought (almost with a smile), that a pupil's throwaway comment could pierce so deep.

***

Annabel had hurried upstairs, conscious that she was

89

slightly upset and rather angry. Room 868 had become a haven for her. The room was empty, which relieved her because she did not feel like talking to anyone. But there was a candle on the teacher's desk.

She walked towards the candle.

"You may light it if you wish."

She turned back to the doorway and there was a man standing there whom she did not know.

"Who are you?" she asked.

"That is not the question that first came to your mind," said the man. "Ask that question instead."

Annabel looked hard at him. "I was wondering how I could light the candle."

"Here," he said. "Use these." And he held out a box of matches. "And my name is Mr English, I used to be the Headmaster here."

Annabel stepped forward and took the matches. She went to the desk and lit the candle.

"Why are you here?" she asked.

"Usually when people want to light the candle I am not far away. And I wanted to meet you."

Annabel sat down. Rex English sat on a desk on the other side of the candle.

"Why?"

"I like people," said Rex English, simply. "And I was

interested in why you wanted to come to this room."

"I wanted to be in a space where I felt I could be myself, a space that would understand. The people I met in room 868 were people with whom I could feel safe. I have a feeling you probably know who these people are?"

Arthur nodded with a slight smile.

Annabel continued: "I did not particularly want to talk to them, but somehow knowing that this is a room where they have been, helps it seem special."

"What was on your mind that you felt you needed the room?" He looked at her very gently. "I know you did not come here to talk. But I wonder, now you are here and the candle is lit, if you are feeling that it might be the time to talk after all. That is why I asked the question, but only answer it if you wish."

"Miss Armstrong's stories about Robin Hood, that there was something there about life, about loss and hope, of cruelty and courage. And songs, and things. And now she has been made to leave." Her voice faded away. She suddenly wondered if she was about to cry.

"You say you like this room, but what you truly like is what this room represents, what it has come to mean to you. What you need to do is think about why you like the meaning that underlies, not simply the room itself. And then you will find the meaning in other places, as well as here."

Annabel was grateful that the man had sounded rather business-like when saying this and had thus helped her not to cry. She did not mind crying at all, but this had not felt quite the right time. "How much do you know about me?" she asked. "And who really are you?"

Rex English smiled. "I am Arthur, Once and Future King. And you are Annabel, and I know a great deal about you. I need good people at the Round Table." He stepped forward and stretched out his hands to her. "Annabel. Will you join us?"

Annabel stood, her eyes still glistening but the tension had slipped away from her face. The room was bathed and glowing from the afternoon sun. Their hands met above the candle flame. "I will join you," she replied.

***

Le Fay was still walking round the school, but by now he was pacing the corridors, thinking hard. He had not wanted to leave the site. They would be trying to win Mordred back, he knew that, but were they playing another game? Was Emma Armstrong important? And there was this other girl...

He turned a corner and there, walking down the stairs, was this other girl. He looked at her eyes and knew he had seen that light before. Much too often. There was no one else in sight. He approached her.

"Little girl," said Le Fay, "I see it in your face: you have been asked to join his strange little group? Before you learn too much more about what it is to be at his foolish little Table I should warn you that I will destroy you and one day I will destroy it. My darkness is greater and deeper than you know and it will consume you."

A figure appeared at the other end of the corridor and walked towards them. Underneath a thick, long, coat something glinted as he strode forward. He stopped and stood next to Annabel, and said nothing.

Le Fay looked at Mr Vincent. But it was Annabel who

spoke: "I do not know who you are, but I know that you see the world wrong. Your darkness is filled not with power but with threats and ignorance. I will not join a group that rules by fear. And finally, in calling me 'little girl' you tell me that you rule by contempt, not respect. I have no time for you. You are foolish if you think you can frighten me. I want to live, I prefer the light."

Morgan Le Fay reached to his pocket. "You give me no choice."

"I am rather old-fashioned," said Lancelot conversationally, stepping slightly forward, "and sometimes carry my sword, purely of course for show. Well, mostly just for show." And his voice hardened. "But I use it when I need." He stepped further forward. "I am too strong for you, Le Fay. I have always been too strong for you. Have you ever wondered why? Let me tell you: first, you are weaker than I am. Second, you are on the wrong side, you really are, and that saps your strength more than you realise."

Le Fay took his hand from his pocket, as if undecided what to do.

"Oh, one more thing," said Lancelot. "A word of advice: never, ever, call an adult: 'little girl'. It never goes down well."

Le Fay stepped back.

"Who am I to spoil the atmosphere of this fine school," he said. He turned to leave and said, looking at Annabel, "But, little girl, I will be back. I am not finished."

"You are finished in more ways than you realise," said Lancelot. "Now go."

Le Fay left.

Annabel turned to Lancelot. "Thank you," she said.

"You did not need me. What you said was enough to protect yourself. Strong wisdom is always the best counter. I do not know if he had a knife in his pocket, but even if he had I don't think he would have dared use it. He does not really like taking risks, for all his threats. You stood well to him; my role was, as ever, simply to unsettle him, annoy him, distract him a little, and remind him of reality."

"I was very scared. I don't know where my words came from. But I stopped being scared when you arrived."

Lancelot smiled. "There, the old man still has his uses. And if one is called to be a school Governor, one might as well do it with a little style." He drew his sword and held it aloft, strong and true. "I am not quite sure I am allowed one of these on site. We better say I borrowed it from the drama department, although, dear Annabel, that is not entirely true."

They both laughed, and walked down the corridor.

Chapter 13

Letting Excalibur Go

Sitting in the room above the café, Jenny Loss was talking to Rex English.

"Do you think Ed will join us?" asked Jenny. "I thought he would, but now I think he is hesitating."

"I don't know what he will do. Glastonbury, and the drive back with Mark, and the welcome back to school, affected him. But so often I have seen people begin to think about their story, their journey, and then delay the decision, stick with the familiar, forget the signs they experienced, remain on the same old path. It takes courage to change. And Le Fay will be offering a good deal to keep him on his side.

"There is often something that the person will not want to give up. To be part of the Table you have to have be willing to want to let other ambitions and desires go. It never happens quickly, and perhaps never completely. But the willingness to want to let go is important. Ed may not yet realise himself what he needs to lose in order to find."

"There is something specific I need to say to Emma. I have asked her to join us this afternoon."

"She told me; I am glad, it would be good to see her. May I stay?"

"Of course."

A few minutes later Emma arrived and joined them at the table.

After the usual greetings Rex English asked: "Do you know what happened to Excalibur?"

"Your sword? Someone caught it in a lake?" Emma answered.

"Yes, but before that, Belvidere couldn't throw it in. Twice I asked him but when he reached the lakeside he became very practical. He thought what an important memento Arthur's sword might be; he thought what a shame it would be for this thing of beauty to be lost. For all sorts of very sensible reasons, he thought he knew better than me. I had to become stern with him and so the third time he threw it in. And it was caught and held in the lake. It is not easy throwing things away, it is not easy knowing the right time to set aside what seems so good, and what has been so helpful. I am wondering, dear Emma, if now is the time for you. Have you the courage to let go?"

"What of? What am I meant to be throwing away?"

"Of the confused sadness and anger you have carried all these years, which, like Excalibur, has a been a weapon that has served you well. It has defended you. In some ways it has been a precious and beautiful thing, but you must now give it away. There it will be received and treasured and held. And you will be free. It is time to make peace with your past. The grief will remain, honoured and deep. You were badly hurt and there is genuine loss, but the confusion, the tension and the anger can go, it is time to hand it over."

Emma looked at him.

And said nothing.

The three companions sat in gentle silence.

"You mean the world to me," said Emma.

There was another pause.

"Trust me, Emma. Let the anger go, throw it far into the lake. Whenever it comes to mind, throw it away. It is no longer precious."

Emma looked up, and the old sparkle and life flashed in her eyes.

"I will do my best."

"Thank you," said Arthur. "You will become an even better Merlin now. And there is someone who would like to see you." He got up and went to the door leading to the corridor to the café. He opened it and disappeared from view. When he came back he was accompanied by Annabel.

"Hello, Miss," she said. "Arthur told me I could meet you here."

"Hello, Annabel," said Emma. "It is very good to see you."

"Please could you tell me what happened to Robin Hood, the next part of the story?"

"Well, I can try. But Miss Loss and Mr English here may not know where we have got to."

Jenny laughed. "Don't worry, we know the stories of Robin Hood rather well. We used to sing them; they were songs before they were anything else. And we will be very glad for Emma to continue. This next part is particularly important."

Emma looked questioningly at Jenny, who gave no sign what was on her mind. She turned to Annabel and began:

Robin Locksley was back in his castle. The true Lord of the Manor was in his right place. The village was content and protected. Guy of Gisborne had gone far away.

Robin ruled with a light touch, guiding and helping as needed, enjoying the company of Friar Tuck, John Forrest, Alan Dale and Will Scathlock. Encouraging and respecting Smith Smithson and those like him, keen to do the right thing by their families and their village.

But there was grief in the air. Many mourned Maid Marian, but none more deeply than Robin himself. He took to walking long distances by himself, whatever the weather. And when he returned he seemed as heavy-hearted as when he had set out.

He set out early one morning and reached some hills, dark in the grey sky. He slowly walked up a rocky path and there, sitting on a stone, was Friar Tuck.

Robin smiled. "I thought I could be alone here, but I am glad to see you."

"You are kind to say so, instead of pretending not to see me and choosing another path, which would have been very understandable. Robin, we are never truly alone. Our thoughts and memories are all about people, living and dead. We are always part of a wide circle, even if we set off at the dawn hoping to leave our friends behind.

"Robin, sit awhile, it is time for us to talk."

Robin saw that Tuck's stone was big enough for them both, and he sat beside his friend. Looking out through the light rain.

"You are right to grieve," said Tuck. "But the grief does not only have to be long walks and deep sighs. It should include remembering with honour and thanksgiving. So, Robin, tell me what we might honour about Marian."

"You know all this: she never put people down. She always wanted to affirm and support. But she was honest, there was no false flattery in her. Respect, that's the word, respect. And she liked people. And she made me smile. And she was brave, very brave."

"You are right, I do know all this. But it is important that we say the words aloud."

The two friends talked long, shared memories and gazed at the brightening view as the rain softened and faded.

The sun rose higher. "It is time to go," said Tuck. "There is work to do."

***

"Thank you," said Annabel.

"Remember," said Jenny. "There is work to do, and that you are valued as you are. Sit lightly on all the pressures, do what you can do, and seek out voices such as Marian's and Tuck's that will support and help you, that are on your side and whose words build you up, not put you down; listen to the right voices. There will be tasks that you can do that no one else can do. You matter."

Annabel was looking at Emma. "Are you okay, Miss?"

Emma looked up and a tear was gently rolling down her cheek. She smiled. "One of the difficult things about being part of this little band" – and she gestured towards Arthur – "is that he is very clever at getting you to do things, or say things, that affect you, let alone the person you are meant to be addressing. He is rather ruthless like that. But, I have to say, it is one of the reasons why I love being part of it. They do tend to take one seriously."

"Thank you for telling the story in the lessons," said Annabel. "It meant a lot to me, and I know it meant a lot to other people, too. It has been very good to have you at the school. Thank you."

"There," said Arthur. "Did you hear that? 'It has been very good to have you at the school'. Ed Moore is unlikely to have said it. If I had said it, you would not quite have believed it. But I think you believe it from Annabel."

"You are quite a crafty old king, aren't you?" said Emma.

"You should hear Lancelot about me when he gets going," said Arthur, with a sigh, and rose to his feet.

Chapter 14

History Need Not Repeat Itself

Ed Moore was restless. He should be feeling content, in several ways he had won: Emma Armstrong had left, he was back on track with Le Fay. Things were running smoothly but he decided to go and see Gary Ladd, and push him to leave. Just to round things off. He wanted to be back in control.

When he arrived in Gary's room he found it empty. On the desk was an envelope, addressed to 'Mr Moore, Headmaster'. Ed stayed standing and opened it.

Dear Mr Moore,

It is time for me to leave. I wanted you to find this letter in this room, and perhaps to read it in this room, because this place has been important to many children at this school. Here they have talked and listened. Poems and stories have been created. In this room Mark Lind began to find his calling and then to share it with others. In this room I asked him to come along to a meeting where he then shared a poem about the Grail. The poem was the one you tore up in this same room a few weeks ago. Why do you hate it all so much? Why the fear and contempt?

For a brief season you stopped the hate, you began to step from the darkness into the light. And then you returned. You went back to Le Fay and all that he stands for. You are losing your wits. You forgot the feeling of Glastonbury. You have lost the gift of imagination, you cannot picture what life around the Round Table is like. Your estimation is lacking, because you instinctively accepted the extra money from Le Fay, binding yourself into deeper servitude to him. You have no sense of the community, no common sense: you do not understand Mr Aldwyn or Miss Loss, or me, or so many others. Can you imagine the Grail? I am not sure you can, so perhaps you have lost that wit, the gift of fantasy, as well. I write this in sorrow, not judgement. It would be a liberation and a joy to you and to many if you became clear-sighted.

The poem you tore to pieces referred to a supper on a Thursday evening, far away and long ago. I mentioned to Mark Lind what you had done and he wrote this new poem, describing something that had happened earlier that same week, but perhaps it has some relevance for our present times.

How much does it cost to sell a life,
to throw a friend away
To cover up the memories
that stirred your soul awake.

How much does it take to lose your way,
to deny what you might be
Thirty coins? Well, that's enough.
Silver? Good, indeed.

Why the anger? Why the greed?
What drives such fear and spite?
Is your pain so deep, so strong,
you can't tell wrong from right?

How much does it cost to close the door,
to shut out the light you see
Thirty coins? Well, that's enough.
Silver? Good indeed.

Thank you for giving me the opportunity to be in this school once again. Travel well, Mr Moore, travel well.

Yours sincerely

Gary Ladd

Ed Moore put down the letter and looked around at the room. He wondered what he would do with it. A large store cupboard might be the answer, stacked high and full, with shelves and boxes with no space for chairs, no space for conversations, no space really at all.

Then he sat and rested his head on the back of the chair. His eyes closed, and his mood relaxed a little; he thought he could hear the birds singing through the window.

He got up and walked out into the fresh air, and was not very surprised when he heard strong footsteps behind him and soon a companion was at his side.

"Let us go and watch some football," said Mr Vincent.

***

Ed Moore and Mr Vincent sat on a bench overlooking the playing fields. From a distance, it would look as if the Headmaster and one of the Governors were enjoying the afternoon sun and pondering matters of school life. But their conversation was rather different.

"In the stories," Ed Moore was saying, "when Galahad finds the Grail, he dies. Is that what he wants, is that what you want?"

"Because something has happened once," said Mr Vincent, "it does not have to happen the same way again. History never exactly repeats itself. Themes may return, patterns may be seen, but the narratives are never quite the same. It is rather a mistake to think that they are, because one then forgets to look at what is truly happening now. We learn from the past, but we are called to fight new battles, not relive old ones. And, if we are trapped by history, there is a danger that we may be tempted to think there is an inevitability about events: that it happened this way then, so it must happen this way now; and thus we can lose our sense of freedom and responsibility."

"So," Ed Moore replied, "to take another example, which I am guessing might be on your mind, just because in the stories Mordred could not see his way through to reconciliation, just because there was a tragic mistake and conflict ensued with fatal consequences, that does not need to happen again?"

"The new Mordred can decide what to do in his own right. There is nothing inevitable about his descent into chaos. We are to learn from the past, not be controlled by it."

Ed Moore shrugged. "If Gary does die, Mr Vincent, that will mean more to you than any of the rest of us. Or is that aspect of the story not being repeated?"

"The theme still holds good. He is as a son to me. I need not tell you more. You are right, I do not want him to die but, whether he does or not in this quest, it is not for me to prevent his calling being fulfilled." He leant forward. "The important thing, Ed, is that you know you do not need to make the same mistakes as Mordred did; you are yourself, you can begin again."

*   *   *

Two days later, sitting on the grass as twilight gathered, in the middle of the ruins of Glastonbury Abbey, Gary waited.

He had found the Grail.

In recent months he had become aware that the false
confidence of previous years had faded to a quiet
acceptance that this was where he was. He was not a
success. Past, slight, glories had come to nothing,
opportunities had been lost.

The loss no longer touched him.

He had begun to be set free when that older memory had
surfaced after so many years. The search for the Grail had
been renewed, the yearning restored. And he was here,
where it was. And in the searching he had learned of
forgiveness and hope, he had learned what it was to be part
of Arthur's dream. Much that was unnecessary had died
within him. He felt content. This was no sudden dramatic
new beginning, more the quiet assurance that this was the
journey. It felt like the closing and opening of different
chapters in the same story, his story, not a different one. It
felt like the flowing of a river following a bend from
dreary and dirty places to fresh, open and sunlit lands and
skies, but it was the same river.

He sensed the music beyond his hearing and knew that his
was now the same song. Or rather that his few notes were
part of the much broader tune. He fitted.

He had found the Grail. It was here.

There was no need to dig it up. It was no longer important
to know that it was here rather than somewhere else. No
need to know what condition it was in after all these years.
And he knew that whenever, wherever, he saw a cup of
wine it would remind him of this. The Grail was truly here,
but it was truly everywhere.

Rex English, Jenny Loss, Mr Vincent and Mark Lind walked across the broad grass towards Gary.

They sat in companionable silence with him. After a time, Mr Vincent asked: "Is all well?"

"All is well," said Gary

"I am thankful."

"Your welfare is tied to mine; your healing helps my healing," said Mr Vincent. He then smiled. "Has anything died?"

"Quite a lot has died," Gary replied, and smiled, too. "It was time for it to do so."

"We shall leave you in peace," said Rex English.

"Thank you," said Gary. "Thank you for everything." And he tuned to Mark Lind: "And it was your poems and stories that first awakened the searching, all those years ago. Thank you."

The group fell quiet. And then the four got up and left Gary where he was. They walked towards the gates of the abbey grounds. Standing there were Emma and Annabel.

"It must be a trick of the sunset," whispered Annabel. "It seems that their clothes are somehow changed, and I keep catching glimpses of light and silver and swords and jewels and robes flickering and shimmering, and, well, I am not sure of the word...."

"Of majesty," said Emma, quietly.

The four drew closer.

"We have just arrived, we hope we are not late," said Emma. "Mr Moore said we could come and find you."

"I am glad he did. In his healing would be my healing," said Arthur, softly. "For similar reasons."

Annabel looked puzzled.

"We are all interconnected," said Arthur. "But sometimes the connections are particularly strong. Dear Emma and Annabel, you are both very welcome. You have arrived at the right time and your presence brings hope. You have had a long journey." He paused and smiled.

"Shall we find somewhere for a cup of tea?"

Lightning Source UK Ltd.
Milton Keynes UK
UKHW02f2006080318
319091UK00003B/55/P